NESSA

3 FOR £1

NESSA

MARGARET DOLAN

First published in 1994 by
Torc,
A division of Poolbeg Enterprises Ltd,
Knocksedan House,
123 Baldoyle Industrial Estate,
Dublin 13, Ireland

A catalogue record for this book is available from the British Library

ISBN 1 898142 01 7

Cover illustration by Rosemary Woods
Cover Design by Poolbeg Group Services Ltd
Set by Mac Book Limited in Stone 10/12.5
Printed by Cox & Wyman Ltd
Reading, Berks

For Sean McCann

CHAPTER ONE

Nearing the city, Nessa saw her grandmother's bed passing her by on the outside lane. She thought she was hallucinating, then she realised it was in a trailer drawn by a jeep, driven by The Ogre. On impulse she decided to follow and moved out into the outside lane, a Mercedes between them.

Why was she doing this, she kept asking herself, and the only answer she could come up with was curiosity or pure unadulterated nosiness. Guiltily she passed the street where she lived. About a mile and a half south of the city, The Ogre slowed down with his right indicator flashing. As he pulled across the street the pedestrian lights changed to red and the Mercedes stopped. Nessa pulled up behind it. Delighted with this bit of good luck, she sat and watched him unhindered.

He skilfully manoeuvered the jeep and trailer, reversing into a place barely big enough to take both outside an olde worlde antique shop painted dark green with *O. O'Shea* written in gold lettering above the window.

The trailer swung dangerously near the headlights of a parked car. Nessa closed her eyes, waiting for the bang. She felt the bang more than heard it. Her eyes flew open. Her front bumper was jammed up against the back of the cream Mercedes. Her heart thumped as she watched the owner jump out, examine the damage and stride towards her. Enraged. Then softening when he saw the terror-stricken white face.

He grinned. "You're a very lucky lady, do you usually stop by running into towbars?"

"I'm sorry, I have no excuse except...." She could hardly tell him she was watching a fellow across the road and took her foot off the brake and hadn't even her handbrake on. "I forgot I was on a slope." She smiled weakly at him. Please God, please don't let *him* see. Too late—he was already beside her.

"Anyone hurt...oh, it's you...are you all right?" he asked with what seemed genuine concern.

Nessa muttered, "Yes."

"Just a bent bumper and damaged pride," laughed the Mercedes owner. He was young and fair and impeccably dressed. Nessa rubbed her neck and wished she could get away. The two men, who seemed to know each other quite well, were in no hurry as they quipped about women drivers and on account of being in the wrong, Nessa listened in silence. She felt she had betrayed her sex by her stupidity and carelessness. But as they droned on, regaling each other with incidents involving women drivers, Nessa jumped out, whipped off her sunglasses and tapping them on the roof of her car said, "Stop right there, I've had enough of your male chauvinism. It was I, Nessa Walsh, all on my owneo, who did it and I'll pay for any damage, OK?"

"Oh, we have a regular little Georgette

Washington here," mocked The Ogre.

"I'm doing a George Bush, actually. *Read my lips*, it's not fair to blame all women drivers for my stupid mistake. The statistics show women drivers are safer, and...."

The Mercedes driver cut in, "Cool it Nessa, there's no damage done...."

"Apart from her vanity," said The Ogre. A shiver ran through Nessa.

"Let me take you for a coffee, Nessa," the fair man said like a caress. "By the way, I'm Terry Horgan."

"No thanks, I'm fine. If you would just push my car back off the towbar I'd be very grateful, I want to go home."

"I think you should have tea first," The Ogre said quietly. "There's...."

"Back off, O'Shea; that fella'd bring you across to his place and you might never be seen again, Nessa."

"I've no intention of bringing her to my place, Horgan," he said icily. "I was going to suggest the coffee shop around the corner."

"Oh yeah, anyway, if anyone is giving her tea and sympathy it's me."

"Thanks, but no thanks...."

Ignoring both as they argued, she went around to see how far the towbar was embedded in her bumper. It wasn't. Her bumper was barely bent. Hardly noticeable. She only had to reverse and leave. She got back into her car, scribbled her insurer's name and address on a scrap of paper, and handed it to Terry Horgan saying, "Sorry for bumping in to you, feel free to claim."

"You can bump into me anytime. May I call you to check if you're all right?"

"No need—I'm fine."

"Here's my card."

"For what?"

"You can call me to see if I'm OK. I might get delayed shock or something."

O'Shea was not amused by this banter, so to irritate him further she said coquettishly, "I might just do that."

Reversing, she just missed O'Shea's feet, then seeing the road was clear, swung the car around in a U-turn and raced off.

Another thing she'd never done before.

What's happening to me? I have a row with a stranger...I follow him home...I crash gawking at him...I U-turn...all because.... Her skin goosepimpled with anxiety at the negative affect this O'Shea was having on her. She'd have to calm down and get a grip of herself...she slowed down...she would never take her eyes off the road again, or be distracted, or follow any man. She felt her face flame with shame at actually following him...it was the bed.... That bloody four-poster...serves her right, she had no business bidding for it.... And then afterwards...the smarmy way he came up behind her saying....

"If you want the bed that badly, you'll have to come home with me and share it."

And when she swung around to confront the deep voice, it was attached to the kind of man she had only read about in romantic fiction. In fact, the kind of hero she thought only existed in romantic fiction. A fairy tale prince.

He straightened to a height in the region of six feet three, give or take an inch, almost taking her breath away. But this Adonis had done her wrong. He had her grandmother's bed. The other bidders dropped out at five hundred pounds but he kept raising her every bid till she conceded defeat at eight hundred pounds, way past her limit. In fact, in her impecunious state, she shouldn't have been bidding at all.

Nevertheless, this man who possessed everything, even her grandmother's four-poster, was about to possess her as well if she wasn't careful. The gold-flecked eyes mocked her, and to protect herself from this man who was too good-looking by half, she said coldly, "I may have wanted it passionately, but there is a limit."

"Oh, and what is your limit?"

"A reasonable price and vacant possession. I don't want any occupants, especially a great lump like you." She smiled sweetly up at him as her body reacted in violent contrast to her words.

"Charming, I see you're well schooled in the art of making friends and influencing people."

"I don't particularly care to make friends with, or influence you, unless of course you're going to give me the bed."

"Had you turned out to be the charming person I expected you to be, I might have considered it. Those curls are exceedingly deceptive. Now it's out of the question. Good day."

As he walked away Nessa said, "Wait...please...."

He turned and came back.

"Well?" he said impatiently.

"It's not just any four-poster...it's special, it was

my grandmother's."

"Really?"

"It has sentimental value." Her voice quivered and she hated herself.

"I'm afraid I'm not into sentiment. I'm a professional and amateurs like you run up the prices with sentimentality. Your type should carry a health warning."

"Nobody asked you to continue to bid—why didn't you drop out? Didn't want to be outbid by a woman, is that it? Or were you hoping I'd hop into bed with you? Do you usually go around auctions buying beds, hoping to fill them with gullible women?"

He laughed. She felt a fool.

"No," he said wearily, "I don't, and no, I didn't keep bidding because I'm a chauvinist pig. I was bidding for a client who gave me a ceiling of nine hundred pounds, and as for asking you to share it with me, that was a *joke*. I wouldn't have a wild thorny thing like you in my bed, anything else?"

"I...I hope it fits into his semi in suburbia."

"Actually, it's a castle in the country, and my client is a lady; a real well-bred one."

Nessa's face blazed, but she couldn't shut her mouth. "I hope my grandmother haunts you."

He smiled. "I'd like that very much, and if you'll excuse me I'll have the bed loaded in case it's vandalized by person or persons unknown who can't graciously accept defeat."

Nessa opened her mouth to reply but this time when her brain told her to shut it, mercifully she did.

He looked her over, staring at her shabby

trainers, her jeans and her mass of auburn curls. "You don't fit the usual over-zealous, over-keen idiots who run up the prices, usually they're well-heeled middle-aged women."

"Is that a fact?"

"Yes it is, definitely not a shaggy-dog little teenage girl who looks as if she's been pulled through a hedge backwards."

She ground her teeth together.

Puzzled, he scrutinized her further. "You look familiar, have I seen you before...on a wanted poster, perhaps?"

Don't answer, her brain said. She clamped her jaws as she glared into his eyes, glinting with amusement.

"Mmm, a unique face, brown eyes blazing with animosity...could do with a nose job for those flaring nostrils. Ah, and a rosebud mouth harbouring sharp little fangs, a vicious tongue and ill-concealed bad temper, just barely under control."

"Well under control," she exploded, "considering I don't usually suffer fools gladly and I've put up with you rabbiting on for ages."

He laughed a deep barrel laugh. "Your grandmother must have been a strange person to leave you a bed that you had to bid for in an auction."

He walked away chuckling.

"It's quite simple really, even an eejit like you would understand," she shouted after him.

Without bothering to look back, he said over his shoulder, "Quite frankly, I don't give a damn."

She wanted to cry and wished with all her heart she hadn't come. What possessed her to bid for the bed? She couldn't afford it at any price, and anyway, where would she put it? It would be totally ludicrous in her flat.

She shouldn't, or wouldn't, be there but for her own stupidity. She had only come to get the little painting, and that shouldn't be there either. If she hadn't been so bloody careless the day the removal men came for her gran's last possessions she wouldn't be in this mess, she thought miserably.

She remembered quite clearly waving her hand, saying, everything, take everything in the room, and they did. Didn't even bother to supervise them. Didn't even miss the portrait till this morning when she idly thought of Gran's bits going under the hammer. The items flashed through her mind: the silver, the glass, the bed, the dressing table...Jeeesus Christ, the portrait, the little portrait of Gran, which stood on the dressing table always...and she hadn't even missed it till now. Shame and disbelief filled her. She'd have to get it back.

Mr Curran, Gran's solicitor, might be able to have it withdrawn. She hopped into her car and drove to the phone box. He was in court. His clerk confirmed the portrait was listed in the auction. Her only hope was to go to the auction and bid for it herself. In her mind's eye she could see Mr Curran tutting "unethical" at her. Well, ethics or no ethics, she was going to get the picture back.

She arrived to find the portrait wouldn't be put up till the following day. Later, after today's auction, she could approach the auctioneer and ask for its withdrawal. She felt light with relief, but then when she saw her grandmother's bed being bid for by strangers a terrible sense of loss coursed through her body and she didn't want anyone else to have it. So she began bidding and couldn't stop.... If she were to be truly honest, the man had done her a favour. A *great* favour. And it had cost him.

They were only expecting six hundred, at the most, for the bed. I've cheated him out of three hundred pounds. Her heart pounded.... Well it wasn't deliberate... she didn't mean to...and she'd told him...if he wanted to make a fuss he could... she'd tell the truth...it might have to go back up for auction.... She wished with all her heart she hadn't done it, but was sort of glad at the same time.... Mr Curran would be vexed.

Mr Curran had shaken his old head when he called Nessa into his office the previous month to discuss her inheritance. Gran's debts were quite considerable in comparison to her assets.

"If we sell everything we might just about break even. You'll be lucky if your inheritance doesn't cost you. Your grandmother was a terrible woman. Always giving. Never prudent."

"That's what I liked most about her, Mr Curran, her goodness of heart. I don't mind not getting anything. She gave me more than enough when she was alive and I'll always be grateful for what she did for me. Anyway, what do I need? I've my degree and teaching diploma, and my part-time job."

"Any sign of a full-time permanent one?"

"Well, I'm on the short list for a teaching post. I've my second interview next month, so wish me luck."

"Indeed I do, Nessa, with all my heart. But I still

wish your grandmother had taken my advice and spent more carefully." He tutted and sighed over the papers. "You know, of course, your uncle Oisín will step in if there are any outstanding debts?"

"No, no, I don't want that, he's too generous. If the auction doesn't bring in enough I'll sell my car and if that doesn't do I'll take out a loan."

Sighing, Mr Curran looked over his glasses at her. "And who would give you a loan, may I ask?"

She looked at him and they both knew the answer.

"You're just like her in every way; headstrong, wilful, as well as being the spit of her...."

His eyes filled with tears and he said gruffly, "I miss her too. A grand woman." Then he tried to cough his embarrassment away.

I'll tell Mr Curran what happened and if he says I've to compensate The Ogre I will.

At least, she thought, I should get the picture without any hassle. Nobody would want a little picture of Gran....

She decided it would be imprudent to approach the auctioneer; he might link the portrait to the bed and call into question her bumping up the price of it. Better keep a low profile.

All the furniture was disposed of the first day. The second would be silver, paintings and glass. She wandered upstairs to check the number against the catalogue before she went home.

The room was a treasure-trove of fine silver, delicate glass and paintings in oil and watercolours. Only a few of the items belonged to her grandmother: a set of silver spoons, a tureen, a

Waterford glass suite and a couple of silver trays, two little water colours and the mini-portrait of her grandmother.

She couldn't find the portrait anywhere. She consulted her catalogue. "Number 5: Portrait of a young lady in oils, painter unknown." She found numbers four and six, but five was nowhere to be seen. Then she found an ante-room where the less valuable goods were displayed. Her heart lurched when she saw the picture being scrutinized by the man who had taken her grandmother's bed. He was examining the initials "FOC" closely with a magnifying glass.

"It's nothing special," she said, coming up alongside him.

Gold-flecked eyes, sharp as flints, turned on her.

"That's your opinion, I happen to think otherwise."

"What I'm trying to say is, the artist isn't important or...."

"You an expert?" he cut in.

"No, but my grandmother told me."

"That the painter was of no account?"

"Not exactly...the painting had no monetary value...it's not famous or anything."

"If she thought so little of it, why did she keep it?"

"Sentimental value—that's her in the portrait."

He looked at it, then at Nessa.... Suddenly grabbing her, he pushed back her hair, baring her face. Nessa stiffened with fright.

"Mmm...underneath that wild and woolly head, remarkable resemblence, every feature cloned except the nose," he said, releasing her. The curls sprang back.

She wanted to yell at him, but couldn't think of anything to say. He held the picture from him.

"Self-satisfied little madam...a real narcissus."

"How can you say that, look at the sweet expression."

"Paintings lie as much as cameras, unfortunately."

"Ah, but look at her eyes, gentle and loving. I think she was in love with the painter."

"Did she marry him?"

"No."

"Why?"

"I dunno."

"I'd say the softness and gentleness were in the eye of the painter who was in love with her and couldn't see the hardness of that curly-headed vamp."

"Now wait a minute you, just who do you think you are, talking of my grandmother like that, a woman you never met, a good, kind, warm human being who never did a bad deed in her life."

"What happened to him?"

"I dunno."

"Didn't she mention the painter whom you maintain she was in love with?"

"She said she knew him long ago."

"I'm afraid my assessment of her stands up better than yours—probably threw him over when a better prospect appeared on the horizon."

Incensed, Nessa said through her teeth, "Surely I would be a better judge of her than you...." Her voice began to wobble. "I knew her all my life, she reared me...do you usually make such rash judgements?"

"I never make rash judgements. In fact, I'm a very good judge of character and this lady was a scheming heartbreaker."

"You can tell all that from a picture?"

"Yes, she was a real Deirdre of the Sorrows."

"How do you know her name?"

"'Deirdre mo ghra' is written on the back...the poor besotted fool."

Nessa, completely frustrated at not being able to defend her grandmother properly, said with a catch in her throat, "If you knew her...she helped everyone selflessly, gave all her money to homeless girls."

"And left you bedless and I presume destitute. Charity should begin at home...."

"But not end there," she shouted at him. "And she didn't leave me destitute, I've my degree and teaching diploma.... I'm a woman of independent means... well, I will be when I get a teaching post and I'm almost twenty-three."

"You do surprise me. You sound more like a bold child, I was waiting for you to stamp your foot and say, 'So there.'"

Oh God, that's exactly how I sound, Nessa thought, squirming with embarrassment.

"Look, dear," he said patronizingly, laying the picture carefully down on a table, "you knew her for almost twenty-three years, what about the other sixty-odd? Perhaps she mellowed in the latter years, atoning for her sins."

As he turned, Nessa slapped his face hard. His eyes glinted like wolves' eyes and through gritted teeth he said, "Go home you silly little girl and stop annoying me, I'm busy."

"Don't sully that picture by touching it again."

"I examine in depth all objects before I bid for them," he sighed wearily, moving on to look over the next painting.

Nessa, disbelieving, said, "You mean you're going to bid for it after what you said...?"

"Yes, while I loathe the narcissistic subject, I admire the artist."

"Well you won't get it," she attempted to say boldly, but the words fractured coming out of her mouth.

"Are you all right?" she heard him ask as she rushed from the room.

She ran till she reached the car. Slumped over the steering wheel, she bawled her eyes out. When the tears turned to hiccups she got angry...then rational.... Everyone who knew her grandmother loved and respected her. Old people, middle aged people, as well as hordes of young girls, all crowded the church for her funeral. And it wasn't only people she had helped in recent years, but old neighbours who described her as the salt of the earth. There were dozens of wreaths and up to a month after the funeral the mass cards were still arriving with letters of condolence.

Nessa tried to persuade herself it didn't matter what this brute thought of her beloved gran, but it did. It mattered very much. She wanted to exonerate her from his vile accusations. A vamp, he called her.

It wasn't even as if he was saying it to taunt her...it was more than that. He hated her grandmother. But why? She couldn't imagine her grandmother having a past. He was right about one thing, she knew very little about her. She knew nothing of her life before her marriage. Had she brothers and sisters? The only one she could ask was Oisín...but what would she ask? She could hardly say, "I met a man who said your mother was a vamp, is that true?"

There was one thing sure and certain—he wouldn't get his hands on that picture. She'd spend every penny she had to ensure he didn't get it. Cheered by the notion of thwarting him, she camouflaged the tear damage with some light make-up, applied some gloss to her lips and raked through her curls with her fingers. She wouldn't mention bidding for the bed to Mr Curran...she was glad it had cost him...served the bastard right.

Refreshed, she started the car. It'd take her about an hour to get home to Dublin. A pleasant drive through the lush countryside of Meath, the Royal County where she lived most of her life until she went to college. Nostalgia gripped her passing Slane Castle and she decided she'd turn off at Ashbourne and go to see the old house. But when she arrived at the boreen leading to the house she stopped at the old oak trees, sat for a few minutes, turned and drove on to Dublin. In her present emotional state she'd probably break down in tears remembering her carefree childhood with her grandparents.

If she hadn't turned off, she'd never have seen the bed...and followed it. She squirmed. If Kathleen did what she had done, she'd have ridiculed her, jeered her, made her a laughing stock. She'd have to put it all behind her, put it down to experience.

After tomorrow she hoped she'd never see O'Shea again.... Oh God, suppose she got the teaching post? The school was only around the corner from his shop...she'd have to pass his place every day.... So what? He was only a man...and if she was appointed she wouldn't be starting for three months. Anyway, she didn't have to say hello or anything.

While she was arguing with herself her stomach groaned with hunger. It was more than six hours since she'd eaten her cornflakes and banana for lunch. She'd have to start eating properly.

She pulled up at the kerb outside her flat. It was a semi-detached ordinary house divided in two flats. Kathleen occupied the bottom and Nessa the top. Putting the key in the lock, a wave of nausea scattered her brain and made cotton-wool of her legs. Climbing the stairs was an effort. Inside the flat, she slumped in a chair till the muzziness passed. Then she went in search of food.

She found two recently acquired cookery books still pristine and unopened. She laughed at herself. Typical; loads of recipes and no food. She rummaged through the presses. A lone tin of beans in the first, another yielded a packet of crisps and a few slices of bread already past their sell-by date, a slightly wrinkled apple and a soft digestive biscuit, plus an empty packet of cornflakes and an almost full tea caddy. The fridge housed a quarter pint of milk, and a bit of butter. Nessa sniffed at both; milk okay, butter not quite rancid. She would have a four-course meal.

For starters, a crisp sandwich; main course, beans on toast; dessert, tea and biscuit, and finish off with the apple. Cheered, she popped the toast under the grill, emptied the beans into a pot and put them to heat on the hob. She then went into the bathroom to freshen up.

As she washed her hands, his face kept coming into her mind. His grave angry face.... She saw herself blush in the mirror, cringing at the thought of following him.

Why, she asked herself again, did she do it?

Before she could answer, she smelt the toast and ran. It was charred beyond scraping and the burnt beans congealed in the bottom of the pot. Another disaster. Was she losing her mind? Was she jinxed?

She stood looking at the mess. Defeated, she turned off the grill and filled the burnt pot with water. It sizzled. She put it out on the window-sill.

She made a crisp sandwich and wolfed it down, then another, eating every crumb. She made tea and drank it with her limp digestive biscuit. It wasn't too bad. Then she ate the perished apple. It had lost its moisture and crispness but it had quite a nice taste.

The doorbell rang as she lay in the armchair, her feet on the coffee table. She jumped up.

Oh God please, please let it not be the landlady... she'll eat the head off me for burning her precious pot and accuse me of trying to burn the house down.... I won't answer.

The doorbell rang, long and shrill.

Knows I'm in, seen the car.... I'll keep her at the hall door.

The smell of burnt offerings followed her down the stairs. She ran back and sprayed her precious

Chanel No. 5 around the room. Running down the stairs in a haze of perfume she fretted at the waste. Her uncle Oisín had given it to her and she cherished every drop.

"You...." she accused.

O'Shea's eyes twinkled. "Glad to see me?"

"No. What do you want?" she asked, livid at the unnecessary loss of her good perfume.

"To bring you these," he said dangling her sunglasses. "They fell off the roof of your car as you tried to run me down."

"I'm not in the habit of running people or things down, even a thing like you. But thank you for bringing my glasses, I'm grateful," she muttered, sounding not particularly grateful. "How did you find me?"

"Kismet.... I was passing through when I saw the mauve and orange metro with a bent bumper and I said to myself, there's Nessa Walsh's car, and then I thought, don't be ridiculous, sure the country must be flooded with mauve and orange metros with bent bumpers and Meath registrations. Why should it be Nessa Walsh's? But I said, what the hell I'll take a chance, and here I am."

"Congratulations, it must have been quite a strain working that out."

"Mmm," he said not listening, "something smells exotic...it reminds of some delicious dish...I can't quite put my finger...."

"Oh, just something I threw together," Nessa said modestly.

"Amazing aroma."

"I'm afraid it's all gone," she said quickly, "but you're welcome to a cup of tea."

"No, thank you, I'm on my way home to dinner."

Relieved, Nessa said sweetly, "Thank you again for bringing my glasses, you shouldn't have gone out of your way."

"I didn't, I was passing.... Were you lost earlier?"

"Lost?"

"When you had your little accident."

"No, why?"

"You were a mile and a half further on from here...."

"What of it?"

"Do you usually add a mile or two to your journey?"

"It's none of your business where I go."

"Unless of course you were following me."

The gold in his amused eyes irked her. A blush warmed her cheek.

She took his hand and patted it tenderly and with downcast eyes said, "Mr O'Shea, you really shouldn't harbour such fantasies, it's not healthy.... Of course there is a faint, very faint, possibility that somewhere out there, there's a woman, an older woman about your own age...desperate enough to follow you home and maybe even try to have her way with you...but quite honestly, I doubt it."

She squeezed his hand reassuringly and looked into his eyes dancing with merriment, "On the other hand, in your case maybe you should fantasize... better than having to face up to reality."

She smiled her concerned smile.

"Thank you, Ms Walsh, for breaking it to me so gently...I appreciate your concern...but you didn't answer my question. If you weren't following me, what were you doing?"

"Normally I would say to a nosy old fart like yourself, piss off and mind your own business, but because you are plainly ill, I'll tell you in simple language that I hope even you will understand. I was timing myself, seeing how long it would take me to get from here to the school around the corner from your emporium, where I happen to be going for an interview later this week. Also to suss out parking facilities in the area.... Satisfied?"

"No, but it sounds feasible.... I'd much rather stick to my assumption you were following me."

Nessa sighed. "You poor thing, you're in dire need of professional help."

"Thank you Ms Walsh, I'll think long and deeply about what you said. Now I'd better go; that exotic aroma is reminding me I'm in urgent need of sustenance."

"Goodbye Mr O'Shea, and thank you again.... Bon appetit."

Walking away he paused sniffing and turning back said, "I've got it...that aroma...it's not Greek or Oriental...it's burnt beans mingled with perfume...how could I forget? As a child, I burnt beans and sprayed my mother's best and only perfume around the kitchen to disguise the smell. For that she boxed my ears."

"How devious of you, maybe it was that beating that unhinged you and turned you into a paranoid misogynist deluding himself he is being pursued by women."

"It's Chanel No. 5 isn't it, with a hint of burnt toast and a slightly more definite aroma of burnt beans."

"Piss off, O'Shea...you're a...a...."

"Yes?"

"A turd!" Nessa screamed, slamming the door in his face. She could hear him chuckling as he walked down the path.

Nessa could now add lies to the defects she'd accumulated in an afternoon.

"That awful, awful man. Look what he's done to me in a few short hours. He's turned me into a lawbreaker, a road hog and a liar."

She had to admit what she minded most was being found out. She hadn't exactly lied about the beans... just a bit careless with the truth...it was he who talked about exotic smells and she just let him. It was his fault jumping to conclusions. It wasn't fair, now that he'd discovered the truth about the meal he'd be less likely to believe her alibi for being in his territory. She couldn't bear the thought of him knowing she followed him.

She scoured the burnt pot till it gleamed, then went in search of food to the corner shop. Returning with the groceries she still got the whiff of perfumed burnt beans the minute she opened the front door. Having showered and washed her hair she went to bed with a book, but was distracted by the events of the day. O'Shea kept coming into her mind. What did the O stand for? Oliver? Ollie? She couldn't imagine him an Ollie...an Oscar maybe.... Or an Owen.... Omar sounded strong, almost arrogant. And he was certainly that.... She slept dreaming of O'Shea.

CHAPTER TWO

Nessa awoke to a glorious June day. Her spirits soared as she looked out her back window. The cherry blossom in the garden almost took her breath away. A tiny breeze nuzzled the rose buds. The birds sang. She opened the window and filled her lungs with the sweet balmy air. She couldn't wait to get out in the garden; a suntrap surrounded by an eight foot wall. She threw on shorts and top, gathered orange juice, bread, butter, banana, pot of tea, pen and paper, on a tray and rushed into the garden.

Heaven...this is my idea of Heaven, she thought, in spite of the tiny little flies who desperately tried to drown in her tea. One succeeded.

Well sated, she watched the swallows darting in and out of the woodshed like they were playing tag. Seduced by the sun, Nessa removed her top and lay down basking in the golden glow.

She became drowsy and almost succumbed to Morpheus as the warm sun caressed her body. Auction...the word made her sit up. She must be prepared. A list. She would make a list...leave nothing to chance...do everything right...she took her up her pen and paper and wrote....

Petrol—she had plenty.

Tyres—pumped up hard, even the spare.

Money—more than enough.

Catalogue—had one.

Nothing else...hardly worth writing down...still, she wanted to do things right.... Time...she nearly forgot time...probably the most important.... She'd leave in plenty of time...leave time for error....

What to wear?

On such a flawless day it would have to be her new white jeans and short sleeved cotton blouse with navy and gold sandals. Reluctantly she left the garden. She'd need just over an hour and a bit to get there, so she'd give herself an hour and a half. She'd be sitting comfortably, well before two, in the auction room.

Coming in from the warm sunshine the house felt colder than usual, a shiver ran through her and her throat felt sore. She showered, dressed, and made herself up. Her eyes watered as she raked through her knotted curls.

Every time O'Shea entered her thoughts she squeezed him out but he kept sneaking back. She had to admit whether she liked it or not he had become a permanent fixture in her mind, irritating her. A man not to be crossed. Yet the danger of crossing swords with him excited her.

She'd be prepared for the abuse and sarcasm that would follow her acquiring the painting. She'd let him rant and rave and be gracious about it. With the picture securely in her possession she'd be courteous and try not to gloat...well...try not to be seen gloating.... Of course he might be charming and civil and shake hands with her and say the best person won. She doubted it. Anyway, she'd be prepared for both reactions. And with sleight of hand, she'd slip in that she'd be in his area the following day for the sole purpose of the interview.

Closing the door behind her, she mentally clapped herself on the back. She was in control. Driving along in the sunshine, her mind strayed to her friend Kathleen in Sardinia. She hoped with all her heart that she was enjoying herself. Especially as she had let her down at the last minute. And Kathleen was very good about it.

"Look, Nessa, it's not your fault you had to cancel the holiday...you're doing the right thing. Anyway," she said, giving a huge guffaw, "I'll have a better chance of getting a fella without you on the scene...no girl should have a friend as good-looking as you, it's not fair...." She hugged Nessa good-humouredly.

It was three days since Kathleen left for Sardinia and Nessa missed her. She'd have liked to have a good bitch about O'Shea with her. Although Kathleen lived in the ground floor flat she spent most of her time in Nessa's. Forever clambering up the stairs to tell Nessa about her latest lover. She was an incurable romantic—always in love, or on the verge of a great affair, or at the end of one. Gran said she was in love with love.... Then again, just as well Kathleen was away. If she heard what O'Shea called Gran she'd more than likely do him an injury.

On the outskirts of Ashbourne, little puffs of cloud appeared. They began joining up at an alarming rate till the sky was completely overcast. A mile or so further on, a fine drizzle began to fall and continued in a misty haze. As she cursed quietly to herself about the unreliability of Irish weather, the car began to veer to the left. A puncture. She felt really hard done by. She'd done all the right things. Why the bloody hell didn't it happen earlier in the sunshine? She could have changed the wheel in relative comfort. Now a wall of very fine rain confronted her and she didn't even have a jumper. The good news was she had time on her side. The jack was tricky to operate. She was going to replace it but as she'd decided to sell the car there wasn't much point.

With difficulty she jacked up the car and changed the wheel. By the time she'd finished she was soaked through. At the next garage on the way she left in the wheel to be mended. The young lad who fixed punctures was reluctantly returning from lunch and was slowly donning his overalls. He was in no hurry and full of chat. Nessa, cold, wet and agitated, said sharply, "I'll collect it on the way back."

"Sure it'll only take a couple of minutes, Miss."

"Sorry, can't wait...."

"Suit yourself, Miss, but it'll be ready in ten minutes."

He was talking to himself. Nessa was already in the car zooming up the road. Chilled to the bone, she turned the heating on full. After a while the car steamed up so much she couldn't see out. She had to open the window and turn the heating down. Drops of cold water dripped from her hair down her back. Her teeth chattered. An over-laden lorry laboriously rumbled along ahead of her, slowing her down and spewing a spray of filthy water on to her windscreen.

On the dot of two she arrived at the auction rooms but couldn't find parking. There were a few spots where she just might squeeze in, but in her present frame of mind she was afraid to risk it. She drove to the very end of the long line of cars and parked. It was now twelve minutes past two. Grabbing her catalogue she ran and prayed it hadn't started on time.

She pushed through the crowded doorway into a space.... Bidding was lively. A silver tray was held up for inspection. She checked her catalogue: numbers two, three, seven and nine were silver trays...but which one...?

"One hundred and ten," said the auctioneer, "and twenty...and thirty...."

"Excuse me," said Nessa to the man beside her.

"Ssshhh...."

"Sorry...."

Bidding was at one hundred and ninety. The auctioneer said, "It's on the market now...who'll make it two? Two, I'm bid...two hundred and ten...twenty...thirty...two hundred and thirty I'm bid...once...twice...three times...to the man in the blue shirt."

"Now, dear, what's your problem?" asked the man beside Nessa.

"What number was that?"

"Six."

"Six...." Her stomach somersaulted...." Number five, portrait of a lady?"

"Sold."

"How much?"

"Ten, only the one bid."

"To whom?"

"Your man over there in the black polo neck."

She knew it would be O'Shea before her eyes followed the man's finger. It was. She squelched over to him. "The picture, will you sell it to me?" she asked bluntly.

His eyes flicked over her. "Been swimming in the Boyne?"

Ignoring the quip, she said, "I'll pay double...treble...fifty pounds."

"If you wanted it that badly, why didn't you bid?"

"I was too late."

"Typical."

"Please, it's very important to me...."

"But not important enough to be on time."

She wanted to hit him.

"I got a puncture," she said as nicely as she could. "I'll give you—"

He cut her short, "It's not for sale."

She could feel the tears gathering at the back of her eyes. "Why?"

"I'm not prepared to answer that. If it was up to me I'd burn it...now excuse me, I'm working."

Nessa tried to stop her face showing pain. Not knowing whether she had succeeded or not, she left the room with as much dignity as she could muster.

Cold and miserable, the aroma of fresh coffee enticed her into an adjoining room where hot drinks and homemade cakes were being sold. A cup of scalding coffee and a hot scone with jam and cream revived her body. Her spirits sagged. There was no point in hanging around now that the picture was in the hands of that rude fiend O'Shea who hated her gran. Her heart contracted with pain. She had let her gran down and she hadn't even got Kathleen to console her.

Things can only get better, she told herself as she drove home. Yesterday was an unplanned disaster, today a planned one. She had to laugh. She was so smug going out today with her list and everything, thinking she had left no room for error. It would do her good, teach her a lesson...learn from her mistakes...better still...blot out the two days and start afresh tomorrow. Who knows, after tomorrow she might even be a schoolteacher. Her spirits upped a notch. Gran wouldn't blame her for not getting the painting and she wouldn't like her blaming herself either. It was no big deal...hadn't she plenty of lovely photographs of Gran, especially the beautiful sepia one in the the silver frame. Even dressed the same as in the portrait. She had given it to Nessa a few weeks before she died.

"Keep it safe, a leana, there's more to it than meets the eye...."

The car began to wobble and go out of control....

I do not believe this...it can't be happening ...another puncture...I must be jinxed.

She pulled on to the hard shoulder. Her only other single puncture had been eighteen months previously. She sat listless, too upset to cry.

So much for optimism, she mused as she got out to walk to the garage. The good news was the garage where she'd left her wheel on the way down was only about a mile further up the road. The bad news was she'd probably be struck by lightning on the way. And feeling as she did, she sort of hoped she would.

She had been walking for about ten minutes in the fine rain when a jeep pulled up beside her. O'Shea.

"I saw your car punctured back there...."

She nodded.

"Can't even change a wheel...want me to do it for you?"

"No, you wouldn't be able."

"Anyone can change a wheel, even a woman."

"Not if there isn't a spare...."

"No spare wheel?"

"It's in the garage further on...I got a puncture on the way down."

"And you didn't wait for it?"

"I hadn't the time...I was in a hurry to get to the auction."

"And you didn't even get there on time, not your day...and wringing wet to boot...what a hopeless creature you are."

"I don't have to take that crap from you...from the minute I first saw you, I knew you were a cruel, sarcastic sadist."

"You mean I didn't fall for your seductive wiles."

"My what? What ark did you fall out of?" she scoffed. "The only thing I wanted from you was my grandmother's picture...to buy...and I was willing to pay way above the odds for it...just...just clear off.... I wouldn't take a lift from you if I'd to walk all the way to Dublin."

"I don't remember offering one."

She walked on with a toss of her head. He drove past covering her in muddy water. She burst into tears; rain and tears mingled running down her face.

Around the corner the jeep stood. The door opened. "Get in," he said. Defeated, she obeyed. The tears continued to stream and she couldn't care less. Her throat ached and she shivered.

"Take off your clothes," he ordered, pulling off his jumper. On impulse Nessa felt for the door handle. He leaned over almost on top of her. His hand tightened over hers on the door handle. Holding his jumper in the other hand he said, "Put this on, you'll get your death." His eyes were kind now and almost sympathetic.

She hated him. She took the jumper and pulled it over her head and began to unbutton her blouse. He looked straight ahead. She began to giggle. If she was in Sardinia now she'd have very little on...might even be topless on the beach. And here she was, fumbling under his jumper, trying to take off her blouse and bra without exposing a glimpse of flesh to someone who wasn't even looking and definitely uninterested.

Wrapping her bra in her blouse, she put them under her seat. Looking down at the floor she said, "Thank you."

The soft cashmere jumper, hot from his body, sent a lovely warm glow through her.

"Take that," he said, pointing to a lovely red tartan rug, "and sit on it."

"I'm OK, really."

"I was thinking of my seat."

She took the rug and wrapped it around her body.

Arriving at the garage he said, "Stay where you are, I'll get it." He returned with the wheel and they drove back to her car in silence. In a few minutes he'd changed the wheel, put the other in the boot and said he'd trail her home in case she got another puncture. She thanked him and got into her car. It was cold and damp and she couldn't stop shivering. He waited till she got a little ahead then followed. She drove like a lunatic all the way home. When she got to the house she decided she'd wave at him and run in and slam the door so he wouldn't be under any illusions. When she pulled up beside the house he sped on beeping as he passed. She felt a bit peaked.

Shivering, she ran the bath, put on all the bars of the fire and all the rings of the hob and her electric blanket. At least when she got out of the bath the kitchen would be warm and as soon as she had eaten she'd go straight to bed with a few aspirins. She had to be well for the interview the next day.

The final interview was between three of them: Danny Farrell, a friend of Nessa's, and a fellow from University College Cork. He had the best credentials but lacked charisma. She could imagine him boring the children to tears while Danny would excite them. He had the gift, a born teacher. And what about herself—what was she?

She'd give them both a good run for their money.

Dropping her wet slacks and knickers on the floor she became shy as the soft wool caressed her body. His half-naked body flashed into her mind sending a rush of pure desire through her. A feeling she'd never experienced before.

"Nessa Walsh, what's got into you?"

The answer she settled for in her feverish state was, it had to be the flu.

A wall of heat hit her as she entered the kitchen, sending the room swaying around her. When the room stilled, she turned off everything except one bar of the fire, poured boiling water into a cup of quick soup, took two aspirins and tried to work out how to get her massive hair pinned up under her jaunty little hat for the interview. For the previous interview the hairdresser had plaited her hair in myriads of tiny little ridges rainbowing upwards towards her crown and perched the hat coquettishly to one side, giving her a suave sophisticated look. Swallowing the soup in careful little sips, each one sending pain shooting through her ears, she no longer cared about her hair and crawled to bed.

Standing in front of the mirror the next day, having slept fretfully and late, she opened her mouth as wide as she could and stuck out her tongue. Her throat, red and angry with yellow patches, was not a pretty sight. Her whole body goosepimpled and she felt rotten. She took two aspirins and heated some honey. The warm liquid slid down, soothing her throat, giving her a lift. After a few false starts and many broken hairpins, she managed to scoop her hair high in a pony tail and wind it into a long curl pinning it flat on top of her head. Having made up her face carefully she dressed in her interview clothes, a rust blouse and cream suit, and put on her little cream hat with rust feathers holding it firm with a couple of her grandmother's hatpins. The feathers were a bit much, she thought, so she plucked them out except for two tiny ones. Apart from her pallor, she looked fine. Before leaving she repeated the aspirin and honey treatment and almost felt well. That evening she would go to the doctor.

"Nessa!" A deep voice called as she entered the school yard. She turned. It was O'Shea striding towards her.

"I hardly recognised you with your hair under control...."

"And the rest of me, is that under control?" she said icily.

"Mmm, yes, except for the temper...that's just about, I'd say."

"Would you now? I'm really glad I met you, you've made my day.... I spent the morning psyching myself up for this interview, telling myself I am the greatest and I have the misfortune to meet you and you knock everything telling me I'm out of control and, and...." Her voice faltered.

"Calm down, Nessa, you look absolutely stunning, cool and sophisticated and in complete control. If you'd listened properly, what I said was your curls are under control."

Yes, she admitted to herself, that's what he said...but.... OK, he was right about the temper.

She mumbled, "Sorry."

"Did you say something?"

She took a deep breath and said in a cracked voice, "I'm sorry. I'm terrified and so nervous, I'll probably make a holy show of myself. I want it so much."

"It wouldn't be the end of the world if you didn't get it, now would it? You're hardly more than a child."

"I'm almost twenty-three," she rasped. "Next month in fact."

"That old? Yes, of course, you did mention it before, time is running out...." His face dead pan, his eyes twinkling.

"You..." she exploded, searching for a something really hurtful to call him, "old man!"

He burst out laughing.

"You're destroying me." Tears stood in pools in her eyes.

"Calm down, Nessa, and don't be so childish."

He was right, she was behaving like an idiot.

"Act at the interview as cool and collected as you look and when they ask you your age say decisively, 'Twenty-three next month and I've loads of experience.'"

"But I haven't. In fact I've only got what everyone else has coming out of college, plus a month teaching English as a foreign language."

"Ever heard of creative CVs ? "

She looked at him.

"Only a suggestion...."

He leaned over, took her face in one hand and gently pushed a stray curl back under her hat. "That's better, it made you look like a little girl not a schoolteacher," adding quickly, "but now you look severe and strong."

She had to laugh.

"There was a little girl who had a little curl right in the middle of her forehead, and when she was good, she was very, very good, and when she was bad, she was dynamic."

A chill ran through her body and she shuddered. He took her trembling hand.

"Are you all right, you're very pale."

"A combination of nerves and flu."

"I'll walk you to the door?"

"No thanks, I'm supposed to look as if I'm in charge, it would look bad if I had to be helped in."

"I suppose it would," he grinned, squeezing her hand.

He looked and smelt gorgeous.

I think I love him, she thought wildly. It's either love or the flu—maybe a bit of both.

"Does he make your knees tremble?" her gran used say.

He does, or it does. If it is love, it's the wrong man. Anyway, he wouldn't look at me. I amuse him. A little liar prone to tantrums. OhmyGod. Is that what I've become? I've known him a few short days, have screamed at him, lied to him, hated him and now, I think I love him. Maybe it's pure lust, she thought feverishly. I want to tear his clothes off. Blushing furiously as she fought for control, she said, "Your sweater, I'll drop it in to your shop tomorrow."

"No, don't. I'll collect it...I pass your place nearly every day."

"Fine," she said.

He must be married. I never thought of that. Her blood ran cold. "Your wife might ask questions?" she asked in what she hoped was a playful offhand manner.

"Why don't you say, 'Are you married?' and I'd say, 'Not at the moment' and then I'd say, 'How about you?'"

"I...I...."

"I hope you're not going to lie...."

"I'm not married."

"Spoken for?"

"No."

"You amaze me...." he chuckled.

Annoyed, she said, "About Gran's picture?"

"It's in good hands," he interrupted. "Even your grandmother would approve."

"Who has...?"

"Coming in, Nessa?" A voice brushed her ear, a hand touched her elbow. She turned. Danny Farrell's eyes danced with devilment.

"In a minute, Danny, we've plenty of time, " she said huskily.

"Nessa, Nessa, how can you do this to me?"

"Do what?"

"Add another asset—that husky voice will slay the selectors."

Nessa laughed. "I've a sore throat."

"A sore throat, when I get a sore throat I sound disgusting."

He eyed O'Shea with a who's-your-man look.

Nessa said nothing.

"Wouldn't you be influenced by that husky voice?" Danny asked O'Shea.

"I hope I'd see beyond a husky voice and pretty face."

"That's the trouble with Nessa, she's not just a pretty face, she's got everything...a beautiful body not to mention a well stocked mind, and now the voice.... I hope when the men are at your feet the women on the panel are at your throat."

Laughing, Nessa said to O'Shea, "He's only saying that because he knows he'll win hands down."

Puzzled, O'Shea said, "Are there only the two of you?"

"No, three."

"How come so few?"

"Ten were called for the first interview and three for the second, we are the chosen few," Danny said.

"Second interview," smiled O'Shea knowingly at Nessa. "I see."

Nessa could see that he saw all right.

"So you've been here before...?"

"No," said Nessa, digging Danny in the ribs as his mouth was forming yes. "We have been interviewed before, but not here, isn't that right, Danny?"

"Absolutely," said Danny loyally. "Second interview, different venue."

Silence stung with lies followed.

"We'd better make a move," said Nessa.

"It's been nice meeting you, I'm Owen O'Shea," said O'Shea, extending his hand to Danny.

"Danny Farrell," shaking O'Shea's hand.

"Good luck, and may the best person win."

"Thanks, see ya," said Danny.

"Bye," said Nessa, boiling beetroot with lies.

"What was all that about?" asked Danny, going into the school.

"I'll tell you when my throat is better. How is Barbara?"

"Pregnant," said Danny flatly.

Completely stunned, Nessa said nothing.

"Told me as I was coming out the door...wish she'd waited till I got back...now I feel so desperate, I'll probably blow it...."

"Nonsense, you probably have it already...you'll beat your man no bother."

"It's not him I'm worried about, it's you, Nessa."

"Who, *me* ? Thanks for the compliment, I'm glad you rate me in the same league as yourself. If I'd thought I was that good I wouldn't have bought my ticket to Australia," she lied.

"Australia—you're kidding."

"No, I'm going to my uncle Oisín...since Gran died there's nothing here for me.... I only came along for the experience...." And with total sincerity she said, "I knew I hadn't a chance against you...you're a born teacher."

"Oh, Nessa," Danny said, relieved, "I'm glad you're out of the running, but sorry you're going away...and you're wrong about me being better than you...."

"Well, I'll pretend to myself I didn't take the job rather than didn't get it."

Danny's eyes filled with love. "Oh, Nessa...I wish...I...."

Nessa quickly discouraged him from continuing. They had gone out together for almost two years. While she was very fond of him, he was crazy about her and was devastated when she told him her feelings. He refused her friendship until last year when Barbara came on the scene. Then they became friends again.

"You'll make a wonderful teacher, the kids will only love ya...." Nessa cajoled.

"I hope so," he said grinning and began to visibly relax.

He was called in as the other candidate arrived.

Nessa sat shivering and sweating alternately.

The hairpins dug unmercifully into her scalp, setting her teeth on edge and aggravating the ache in her throat. She longed to pull them out but felt she should persevere. I could have stayed in bed, pampered myself with warm honey and a good novel, she thought miserably. Am I as good as Danny? Have I underestimated myself? I'd love to find out...go for it...and if chosen, decline.... But if I was offered the job...would I have the willpower to turn it down? Maybe I'd start making excuses and take it.... I'd never sink so low...not with Barbara pregnant and all that....

She decided not to take the risk in case she'd be found wanting. Next time, next time she'd go all out for it. Be single-minded. At least next time she wouldn't have to consider Danny and Barbara. She thought again of Australia. Should she turn her lie into the truth and go?

Her uncle and family were always asking her over. She only had to say the word and he'd even send the ticket. She loved them all and felt loved by them. Apart from Kathleen there was nothing to keep her here and she could more than likely persuade Kathleen to come with her. So why not give it a try? There was just one other consideration. Owen O'Shea...her heart beat wildly when she thought of his teeth, his smile...his eyes twinking kindly...but what about his dark side? Where her beloved gran was concerned he was cold and bitter. He didn't try to conceal it. Made an issue of it in fact.

When he was kind he reminded her of someone...something about his mouth or the way he moved his head...it wasn't his eyes, they were uniquely his own.... Anyway she could hardly love someone who hated her gran. Maybe it was pure lust she felt for him? She blushed when she thought of how her body reacted to him. She imagined most women would react in the same way. And what would he think of her, if he thought of her at all, following him and lying about it? Burning food, and if not exactly lying about it, deliberately concealing the truth. And now—not only obviously lying about being here before, but getting Danny to lie too. And she'd lied to Danny too. Was she becoming a habitual liar? Does one suddenly become a liar?

Once, only once, as a child, she remembered telling Gran a lie—said she had a pain in her stomach when she didn't want to go to school.

"You shouldn't lie, Nessa, you haven't the face for it."

Gran was right, even Owen O'Shea knew each time she lied.

Danny came out beaming and whispered to Nessa, "I think I've got it." Nessa was delighted and said she knew he would.

"I'm glad you had already decided to go to Australia before I blurted out about Barbara, I couldn't bear to think you stood down because you felt sorry for us."

Another lie was about to roll off her tongue. Instead she said, "If I'd known you held me in such high regard, it might have been a different story." Then the lie rolled, "Anyway I rather fancy teaching little Aussies."

Then the lie turned into the truth as she thought, I would fancy teaching in Australia.

"And the dynamic O'Shea, where does he fit into the scheme of things?"

"Nowhere that I know of," she answered truthfully.

Danny closed one eye and surveyed her critically, "Oh yeah?"

Luckily she was called in at that moment.

"Don't let's lose touch—I'd like to see you before you go away."

"Ring me at the bookshop Friday or Saturday."

"Still phoneless in flat-land?"

"Can't have everything."

"And you, Nessa Walsh, have everything else."

"Thanks, you're very good for my ego."

"I only tell the truth—you are the most beautiful girl in the world."

He hurried away. Nessa sighed deeply and went in to be interviewed. The interview was short. She told them she was no longer interested in the position and they thanked her for coming.

Outside she unpinned her hair and shook her head. Her curls sprang out with luxurious abandon making her almost lightheaded with relief. As she drove around the corner she noticed O'Shea's jeep was no longer parked in front of the shop. Without thinking, she pulled into the empty space.

Just a little peep in the window, she told herself.

It was quite dark within and she couldn't see very well. Curiosity overpowered her and she went inside.

CHAPTER THREE

A bell tinkled as Nessa entered the shop. Coming in from the sunshine, it took a while for her eyes to adjust. It was a very long room housing an exquisite stock of antiquities. The silver in glass cabinets almost took her breath away. The place was still, like the Marie Celeste; everything in order but no one around. O'Shea would hardly leave the place open.... Suddenly in the gloom she saw a person sitting behind a desk at the very end...O'Shea? Her heart began to pump great whorls of blood through her veins. Imagine being caught in his den? If she attempted to sneak out, the bell would probably clang all over the place and she'd be caught...maybe he'd chase after her thinking she was a thief.

Oh God, she thought, if only I'd minded my own business...the only thing to do is brazen it out...pretend I want to buy something...he can't prove.... What'll I ask for? Something small...a silver teaspoon....

She moved slowly towards the figure at the back of the shop, her heart swinging out of control, weakening her progress.

She came face to face with an old man dozing in a rocking chair. His skin was like crinkly parchment. A moustache, grey spiked with gold needles, fringed his mouth like a rough yard brush. He drooled tiny pools into his waistcoat.

Creep out. That'd be the best thing.... Creep out and hope the bell won't wake him...even if it did, he'd hardly give chase, but it might give him a fright, a heart attack even.... OhmyGod, if only I wasn't so bloody nosy.... Backing away on tip-toe she began her retreat watching the old man who snored and snorted and seemed on the verge of waking and catching her any second. The picture of Gran caught her darting eye. It stood on the desk opposite him, its frame newly polished. Was he the customer? Why would he want a picture of Gran? She peered into his face...a slightly familar look...a touch of O'Shea...she half closed her eyes and squinted at him...a bit of a resemblance, but not a lot.

He shuddered awake, terrifying her. She decided not to run...less anxiety for him when he'd see she was harmless.

Gazing at her, bewildered.... "Deirdre," he said full of wonder, "It's you!"

She said softly, "I'm Nessa...Nessa Walsh...I'm sorry to disturb you."

He whitened, looking at her long and hard.

"I was having a little browse...." Her voice trailed as she watched him. He looked at the portrait, at her, at the portrait and back again. Their eyes met.

"Yours?" she said nodding at the picture.

"Yes, a surprise present," he said, taking it and rubbing it with his sleeve before tenderly placing it back on the desk. "And you, what are you doing here? Or as Bogey might have said, of all the antique shops in all the world, how come you picked this one?"

"Well, I can't pass an antique shop without...and I was sort of following the portrait...I went to the auction specifically...."

"And you were outbid by Owen?"

"Something like that...Deirdre...my grandmother...."

Sadness edged his smile. "I can see that—you're the spit of her...."

"So everyone says...."

"And rightly so.... She was my fiancée."

"Fiancée?"

"Yes, and I was that painter...Fionn O'Connor," he said proffering his hand. Nessa shook it warmly. He looked lovingly at the picture. "And madly in love with Deirdre...."

"O'Shea?" she asked, not knowing what to say.

"My grandson," the old man said proudly. "You know him?"

"Not exactly, saw him briefly at the auction."

"He didn't say."

"Well, we were only bidding against each other...." Lies queued up ready to roll off her tongue. "I saw him more than he saw me...I was at the back and could see him...he couldn't really see me...."

"That makes sense, if he saw you I'm sure he'd have made the connection. Might have even dragged you back here with him to surprise me.... Owen nearly knows as much about Deirdre as I do, I talk a lot about her, probably too much..... But how did you find this place, did you know about me?"

"No, it was chance, I was in the area. Saw the name and just came in."

Stop before your lies catch up with you, she warned herself.

"Imagine that...I was so pleased he found the painting. So sad she was gone. You know, I never thought of that. I never thought of her being dead.... I found her too late...."

The words trembled on his lips and tears stood in his rheumy eyes.

"Will you join me in a cup of tea?"

Nessa hesitated, thinking of O'Shea. He clearly didn't want them to meet, specifically told her not to come here, not even to return the sweater. What if he came back?

"I really shouldn't," she said.

"Humour an old man who desperately wants to talk about the love of his life. It was a terrible shock finding out she was dead. I had been hoping...."

She knew he was manipulating her, playing on her sympathy, but you'd have to be a hard-hearted Hannah to resist those pleading eyes.... O'Shea loomed large in her thoughts. How would he react? While he told Fionn about her grandmother's death and brought him the picture, he didn't mention he'd met her and he was very definite she shouldn't enter the premises...but still, when he sees she had no detrimental effect on the old man, in fact just the opposite, he should be glad. Of course he would. Wouldn't anybody? And if he isn't? What the hell. What can he do if he finds me here? Bawl me out no doubt—worth the risk if it pleases the old man.

"OK."

"Good girl. Will you lock the door while I make it...it was supposed to be locked...I forgot."

"Where's the key?"

He handed it to her, delighted.

"Now," he said, as they sat together with a mug of tea each, "tell me about your grandmother."

"There's not a lot to tell, even though Gran reared and loved me dearly, she was a very private person.... I really don't know an awful lot about her, except she was good and kind and helped everyone especially homeless girls and unmarried mothers. She even left the house to them as a refuge...."

"That's the sort of thing I'd expect of her, she was a kind soul. Do you know anything of her before and around the time of her marriage?" he prompted.

"She never mentioned her family at all...I don't even know if she had brothers and sisters."

"She had one sister, Maura, thin and bitter as a lemon...."

"I asked Gran once what her mother was like and she said, 'Hard, very hard,' and changed the subject. I know she had an aunt Nessa she was very fond of. I'm called after her. She stayed with her in the country—Mayo."

"Mayo, so that's where she was."

"I think that's where she met Grandpa. He was a Mayo man, a doctor. They had two children: my uncle in Australia and my mother. They lived first in Mayo, then in Ballsbridge. They seemed to have been a happy family."

She paused. He watched her intently, willing her to continue.

"My mother died when I was four. My father took her death badly and began drinking heavily.

I went to live with Gran and Grandpa. He died when I was ten. The medical term was cirrhosis of the liver. Gran said he died of a broken heart."

"I can well believe it.... Was she like Deirdre...your mother?"

"Yes, very, except her hair was straight but she had her nose. The lucky thing."

"Yes, it was a very good nose," he laughed.

"I really only remember my mother through photographs and Gran telling me about her...."

Why am I doing this? Rabbiting on telling family secrets. Close your big mouth, she warned herself, but suffering from acute verbal diarrhoea, eagerly answered when Fionn said, "And your father?"

"I don't feel I knew my father at all.... Sad brown eyes.... The thing I remember about him most was his smell...everytime I get a whiff of whiskey I see him swaying, smiling beseechingly...not a good memory of my father...."

"The loss of love is a sad thing...pity he didn't find another soul-mate."

"Gran said he was a one-woman man so he sought comfort in the bottle."

He sighed. "I didn't look at a woman for ten years after Deirdre...always hoping...."

Afraid he was going to break down, she rushed in with more information.

"Soon after that Grandpa retired and we went to live in Ashbourne."

"What was he like, your Grandpa?"

"Lovely, gentle, good-humoured...daft about Gran, always buying her flowers and little pressies. She said he was too good, had her spoilt rotten. My mother's death had a terrible effect on them."

"It would of course."

"Gran said Grandpa lost his sparkle when she died but regained it with me. She said I made up for their terrible loss. I always felt wanted by them...I really had a lovely childhood, I was very privileged."

"And your uncle?"

"He's in Australia years and years, before I was born. I went out to him a few times with Gran and Grandpa and he came home often. Grandpa, when he retired, was always popping off to Australia to visit Oisín."

"Oisín, your uncle is called Oisín...."

"Yes...."

"What was your grandfather called?"

"Sean."

Almost in a whisper the old man said, "And she called her son Oisín."

He gave her a sad smile...a familiar smile.... Oh God...I don't believe this...she leaned over scrutinizing him...he couldn't...he was...no.... I'm hallucinating...the fever coupled with an over-active imagination was distorting her rationale ...sure wasn't she always adding two and two and getting ninety-six.... Everyone said.... She blinked repeatedly...then looked closer, examining ...the truth was staring her in the face and she didn't want to know...she looked away and back again...it was like as if her uncle Oisín's face was superimposed...an older face but the same features.... Uncle Oisín lined, with a moustache.... Oh God, I don't want to know..... Serves me bloody well right...if only I wasn't so curious.... What to do? I could tell O'Shea....

She shivered at the thought.

Fionn looked as if he was going to weep, so Nessa added with a laugh, "And my mother, Niamh...*and* the house was called Tír na nÓg. All my bedtime stories were of Fionn Mac Cumhaill and the Fianna."

He regained his composure.

"She always loved Celtic mythology...me too.... I said I'd take her to Tír na nÓg...but she pointed out, it was Oisín and Niamh who went to Tír na nÓg not Fionn and Deirdre...and the night we parted she was so sad she said she hoped she wouldn't become a Deirdre of the Sorrows. I hoped so too...I was definitely Fionn of the Sorrows for a long time...Oisín...she called her son Oisín.... Did she ever mention me?"

"No, not to me."

His face fell.

"Well, not that I remember."

"I had hoped she cared."

"Just because she didn't tell me doesn't mean...she told me nothing of her past at all.... I didn't even know she had a sister...and she loved the portrait, it stood on her dressing table always...."

"On her dressing table...all those years, maybe she didn't forget me after all...."

How could she, Nessa thought, with Oisín a permanent reminder? And yet what about her grandpa and uncle? They had a wonderful father-son relationship.... She had often remarked on it to Gran who just smiled and said it was unique. And Fionn clearly didn't know about his son.... Could she possibly be mistaken, after all, isn't everyone supposed to have a double? She looked closer, hoping...there was no mistake...but where did that leave her? Burdened with this terrible secret.... Does uncle Oisín know, and what about Grandpa ...did he...? Hardly...the rapport.... Maybe Grandpa thought.... Oh God! Gran wouldn't...she couldn't pass him off...unless she was two timing...she wouldn't...definitely not...not her Gran. Look at the way she looked at Fionn as he painted her...it was plain she loved him madly.... God, was she the only one who knew? Should she tell her uncle Oisín...write and say I met an old man who painted Gran's portrait. Said he was engaged to be married to her and still seems to be in love with her memory. By the way, he looks a lot like you.

Her mind was freewheeling...she felt dizzy...her throat was radiating pain through her ears. She closed her eyes. "Curiosity killed the cat...." that's what Gran used to say to her when she was a child....

"You all right, my dear...?"

"Not really, I have the flu...I'd better go...." Her throat tightened.

She felt feverish...her stomach woozy...her chilled skin prickled.... Maybe if she had something to eat...but she wouldn't be able to swallow....

He fished inside his waistcoat pocket and took out two tablets in foil. "Take these, they'll take down your temperature...."

He gave her the tablets and a glass of water. She took them. She could feel them stuck in her throat making her feel bilious.

"Yes," he said, "the night I left for London to make my fortune...Deirdre said she'd love me forever and I said I'd love her forever. I kept my side...I thought I'd be like Dick Whittington...make my fortune in no time...come back and marry Deirdre. It was the worst of times, the Thirties...I humped around my portfolio.... Nobody was interested. I got the odd day's casual work on building sites. Staying in cheap hostels. I wrote every day...she couldn't reply because I was moving around so much...at last I got a job draughting in an architect's office and moved into cheap digs. I was ecstatic, an address at last. I wrote immediately. Waited. The thought of hearing from Deirdre filled my heart to bursting...a week...two weeks passed...I blamed the post...the landlady...I sent a telegram...reply, gone away.... My brother Padraic who had lived in Dublin for a few months had gone back home. I wrote to him and asked him to go up to Dublin and call on Deirdre. He called. Her sister said she'd gone away and wanted nothing more to do with me and to stop bothering them. It took me weeks to save for my fare home.

"I went straight from the boat to the house. I must have looked a sight. I knocked and knocked on the door. I may have even kicked it. Nobody answered.

"I began watching the house. Her father came and went. Her sister and her mother, too, but no Deirdre. I thought they were hiding her. Then I got it into my head they'd murdered her.... As you can see I was losing my grip on reality. I went to the police station and reported her missing, presumed killed by her family.

"They investigated. They were very kind and told me she was fine and was staying with an aunt in the country. They wouldn't say where. They said she didn't want to see me any more. Six months, only six months since we parted and she didn't want to see me.... The Gardai contacted my family. Padraic took me home to Kerry. I think I had a nervous breakdown...nowadays I would have been treated...counselled... but sure now or then nobody can mend a broken heart.

"My mother wrote to Deirdre, pleading with her to even write to me and tell me she no longer cared. There was no reply. Padraic, a small farmer by birth but not by choice, suggested we emigrate to Canada. We already had two sisters there. I was still hanging on to hope.... My mother, who was a townie, jumped at the idea, saying it would suit all three of us.... I wrote again to Deirdre...no reply.... I didn't care where I was, so I went to please my mother...and she me...both of us doing what we thought was best for the other.... As it turned out it was very good for both of us.

"My brother-in-law got me a job in commercial art. I loved it and threw myself body and soul into the work. I hated Deirdre for a long while. I wanted to confront her...if I had an address sooner maybe I'd have got a Dear John letter...at least I'd have known.

"After I had gone as far as I could go in Toronto and was asked if I'd like to start up a branch in Ontario, I accepted. You know this may sound crazy but as soon as I reached London, Ontario, I had this terrible urge to find out about Deirdre. I had to know...wanted to know desperately.... I asked the Salvation Army to trace her. They did. Married with two children. The pain, even after all that time, was unbearable. I couldn't believe it.

Married with two children.

"I met and married Connie just before the Second World War started. A loving, good woman...a nurse at the local hospital. We were great friends and when our friendship turned into courtship I told her all about Deirdre. She said she felt I had enough heart to accommodate both of them, but she wanted at least half. In time she had almost all. But there was always a corner.... I couldn't forget Deirdre...and since Connie died, Deirdre has taken over most of it again. I still can't understand how Deirdre could do that to me. Do you, Nessa?"

"No, I don't, it doesn't sound at all like Gran...maybe her family put pressure on her.... From what you say they weren't exactly mad about you."

"They hated the sight of me. 'Artists die of poverty in the gutter,' was her mother's only remark when Deirdre introduced me."

"They must have had a row, she seemed totally alienated from them, never mentioned them. I never even saw a picture of her mother or didn't even know she had a sister. She had one old sepia photo of her father."

"Not even in her wedding photos?"

"No, none of her family are in her wedding album except her aunt Nessa."

"That's odd, I thought they'd approve of a doctor."

"It is very peculiar...even if they did put pressure on her I couldn't imagine Gran yielding, she had plenty of spunk...it's so unlike her."

"That's what I thought...if she was flighty...I gave her a ring with my heart that night, an opal."

"With little seed pearls like petals?"

"Yes that's the one."

"I thought Grandpa gave it to her. She never left it off, the stone used to turn black when she was ill."

"There was a superstition opal was unlucky but it was her favourite stone.... Have you got it?"

"No...I've none of her rings, not even her engagement ring.... I made Oisín take the wedding ring...he didn't want to...said he only wanted photographs and papers...along with her wedding ring they were the only pieces of jewellery she had left.... Towards the end she was running out of money so fast she could have sold them...sold nearly everything to look after her girls...."

"A good cause." He looked lovingly at the picture. "Is that not the face of a woman in love...?"

"Yes...." Nessa croaked.

"I was too weak, gave up too easily.... I should have sought her out, fought for her...taken her. Nobody would do that to Owen, he's a tiger...the meek do not inherit the earth, my dear."

"He's aggressive all right."

Fionn looked at her questioningly.

"I mean he looks like he might be aggressive."

"No, no, not aggressive; strong, but fair...."

Shivers crept through Nessa's clammy body. If she didn't move soon she'd never make it home. She stood up swaying a bit.

"Are you all right?"

"Just miserable with the flu...." her voice squeezing through her closed throat.

"Stay my dear, Owen will be back soon and will drive you home."

"No, no, I'll be okay. Have my car outside."

Stiffly he stood up, dwarfing her even though he had quite a stoop.

"It was very painful...but comforting to know Deirdre lives on in you," he said, his eyes blurred with tears.

Nessa wanted to hug him, take away the pain her grandmother had caused. He walked her to the car.

"Please call again, I'm usually here Tuesdays and Thursdays. The rest of the time I spend in Wicklow with my daughter."

She got into the car trying to look lively as the old man waved her off. Luckily the traffic was light and she slid out quickly. She'd be home in no time. Her stomach felt queasy. She drove slowly.

Why did Gran do it, she asked herself over and over. This lovely old man loving her grandmother all this time. She could understand Owen's bitterness on behalf of his grandfather. She'd probably feel the same if her grandmother had been so cruelly wronged. But she couldn't believe her gran would deliberately cause such pain and sorrow.

At the red traffic lights she rested her head momentarily on the steering wheel, then straightened immediately...someone could think she was drunk. Anyway, only a mile and she'd be home in bed. Bed.... The four-poster swam tantalizingly in front of her...but any bed, even her hard little divan, would do very nicely. The lights changed to green, the car stalled. A blast from a car horn made her jump. She revved, the car roared. Another blast. She looked in the mirror preparing to give two fingers. Nobody behind her.

It was O'Shea in the jeep, going in the opposite direction, hooting at her. He winked, smiled and was gone. His smile stayed on her mind all the way home.

She heard the tyre hissing out air as she roughly bumped the kerb outside her flat. Never was she so grateful to see the place. Shivering in the afternoon sun, she drank a glass of water and fell into bed fully clothed. Her good suit, her only suit, would be ruined.

To hell with it, she thought, then rising slowly took all her clothes off and laid them on the floor. With her head buzzing she fell into a nightmare. Noise everywhere including the tinny sound of the door bell shrieking. She awoke, listened, definitely the doorbell in a long banshee wail. Her eyelids drooped and on a wave of nausea she was sucked back into the black sleep. All night long the noise of traffic rolled. Horns hooting, alarms ringing, bells clanging. Faces magnified and distorted swung in on her.

She woke in sunlight shivering in the damp sheets. Even the duvet was wet with sweat. Her tongue dried out, stuck to the roof of her mouth, her throat like sandpaper. She felt too ill to get to the kitchen to get a drink.... The buzzing started up in her head again, forcing her to realise she had to get help or she'd be found dead, decomposing, smelling to high heaven by poor Kathleen the following week....

She shook at the thought. She'd do it in little stages...first step...out of bed, then the kitchen, no, dressing gown second, she could hardly crawl naked down the street...so first out of bed, second the dressing gown, third the drink, fourth the stairs and fifth the hall door.... All she had to do was do it slowly and not panic. The thought of her decomposing body spurred her on. Shivering she held on to the taps as nausea enveloped her.

The buzzing in her ears elongated to a piercing ringing...it got louder, recognisable...it was the doorbell, definitely the doorbell. Half past eight. Nobody ever called at half past eight. It was a miracle. Someone up there likes me, she thought, as she negotiated the stairs, clinging to the bannister, praying who ever was there wouldn't go away. The bell buzzed incessantly.

Luckily, she thought, whoever was there was as anxious to get in as she was to let them. Even the landlady would be welcome.

Pulling the door open took all her strength and she almost fell out on O'Shea, standing big and strong in the jamb of the door. She could have cried with joy. She put out her hand to him. He knocked it away.

"What do you think you're playing at?" he demanded.

His face came in waves, ugly, menacing, his eyes wild. She swayed forward. He grabbed her, pinning her against the wall.

"Spare the theatricals. I want to know what were you doing snooping around my place behind my back, upsetting an old man, you nosy little bitch."

She couldn't answer, her voice wouldn't work. He let her go. She slumped forward, feeling the buttons of his shirt scrape her face as she slid to the ground.

When she opened her eyes to a big open-pored face with a red-veined nose and white-lashed eyes, inches from her, she tried to scream. A jagged rasp tore her throat.

"You're all right pet, you're safe in your own bed," said the big rubbery lips as the jowls flapped. "I'm the doctor, Paddy O'Brien. O'Shea brought me. Here, sip this."

Lifting her gently he held a glass of water to her cracked lips. She was wrapped in a familiar yet unfamiliar rug. She'd seen it before.... When she saw O'Shea she remembered.... It was his. Her damp duvet and sheet were on the floor. He moved nearer. Instinctively she cowered, putting up a shaking hand as if to ward off blows.

"Nessa," he said gently. "Oh, Nessa."

She began to whimper. She tried to tell the doctor to send O'Shea away but the words wouldn't form. She felt so weary she gave up trying. The doctor gave her an injection. Their voices came in waves.

"She's very ill. If she had someone to nurse her I could leave her here and come daily, otherwise I'll have to move her to hospital...family?"

"None as far as I know, except for an uncle in Australia."

"Fat lot of good he'd be to her."

"I could take care of her...I mean get someone to...."

Nessa attempted to sit up, shaking her hand and head as vigorously as she could. Then fell back on the pillows, exhausted.

"There, there, pet," said Doctor O'Brien, "don't fret, you don't have to do anything you don't want to. Is there anyone I could contact for you?"

She shook her head.

"Right so, I'll just go and ring the hospital...."

Hospital, someone must tell Kathleen, she thought, but couldn't say anything.

She tugged the sleeve of his jacket.

Misinterpreting her anxiety, Doctor O'Brien said, "Don't worry, pet, I won't be long. Have a phone in the car, O'Shea will mind you."

"Yes of course. You'll be quite safe."

O'Shea sat down beside her and tried to take her hand. She pulled it away.

"I'm sorry, Nessa, the old man was very emotional when I got home. He was the reason I didn't want you to go in.... I should have told you. He was crying, said you called. I was annoyed and when you wouldn't answer the door last night...well, as you see I've a terrible temper."

She tried to form the word sorry but it wouldn't come out...she tried again, "Sor...." and the rest petered out. She began to weep, great mournful sobs. She couldn't stop.

The last thing she heard was O'Shea saying, "Please don't, Nessa," as she was sucked into the black pit of unconsciousness.

Voices crowded in on her, shouting at her, mouths curled, accusing her, faces zooming in.... She tried to escape from them...but she couldn't move...desperately she fought to free herself, but she was tied down. Her eyes flew open.

"Take it easy, love, you'll do yourself an injury," the doctor said, holding her shoulders. "You're in the ambulance on our way to the hospital...terrible bumpy...that's why you're strapped down...just as well the way you're thrashing about...."

She wanted to thank him, at least smile at him...but she didn't know whether she succeeded or not.

Nessa drifted in and out of sleep, conscious she was in hospital, feeling safe. She awoke, the sun streaming through the window, the room full of flowers. She felt much better. The noise in her head was gone and she could swallow.

The nurse came in. "Back in the land of the living, Nessa? Your fella's been here twice yesterday armed with acres of flowers as you can see...."

"I haven't got a fella," Nessa croaked.

"Well, this fine thing keeps hovering around. Saw him talking to your doctor a few times, like they were mates."

O'Shea, that bastard O'Shea.

"Please, take them away, I don't want them. And don't let him near me."

"OK, OK, take it easy, I'll take them out when I'm going and I won't let him in if that's what you want.... I'm going to sponge you down and tidy your hair, it's a bit out of control."

Out of control...that's what O'Shea had said.

"You can cut it off if you like," Nessa said despondently.

"We won't have to do anything that drastic. I'll brush it as gently as I can and plait it, OK?"

"Righto."

The nurse sponged her down, gave her a fresh nightdress and chatted about holidays and weather as she plaited her hair. Nessa told her about Kathleen being a nurse and that she was in Sardinia. It turned out they had trained together.

"Dublin is like a village. Everyone knows everyone or at least has a mutual acquaintance," the nurse said. Nessa agreed.

Doctor O'Brien called.

"Howya?" he said, good-humouredly.

"Fine," she said.

"If you make sufficient progress you'll be out next week, but you'll need looking after. I can't send you home to an empty flat without even a phone. I'll see about a convalescent home."

"No, no please, Kathleen will be home, she'll look after me, she's a nurse."

"Who's Kathleen?"

"My best friend, more like a sister. My grandmother fostered her for years. We share the same house. She can cook and everything. Makes great dinners. Anyway, I have no money. I can't even afford this room."

"Will ye stop frettin', you're in as a public patient. The public ward was full and this room was free and you needed a lot of rest. No cost. If it's needed, you'll be turfed out."

"That's a relief, thanks."

"You're a terrible worrier...anything else bothering you?"

"Yes, I'd be very grateful if you would ring the bookshop, ask for Sally and tell her I won't be in on Saturday. It's only a day a week but I can't afford to lose it."

"No problem, name and number?"

She told him.

"'*Fíos*,' know it well. Must and dust...great place ...an old haunt of mine when I was a student...Brian...Brian Murphy, great character, used to run it."

"He died—left it to his niece Sally."

"Good to see it's surviving."

"Just about."

"Often used to root around it...got some great bargains...still have them.... Would you like some books?"

She nodded.

"Heroes rescuing maidens in distress—that sort of thing?"

She was about to say that was the last thing on earth she wanted to read, but looking at his kindly beaming face, she said, "Thanks."

He went off humming.

Her mind freewheeled over books...people.... Brian...the day he interviewed for the Saturday job four years ago. Only interested in what she read. Only talked books. Handled them reverently.

"You can sit on a chair and go anywhere with a good book; back into antiquity, forward ino space, a book is like a time machine," he said. His treasured books were kept in a magnificent bookcase in the back room. One was an old bible he picked up at a car boot sale for five pence.

"A shilling, imagine getting that for a shilling," he said, fondling the fine leather cover, cracked with wrinkles like his old walnutty face.

He was dead almost two years. Sally, almost as much in love with books as Brian, had to sell a lot of the treasures from the bookcase to keep afloat.

Exhausted but relaxed, Nessa eventually fell into a long, untroubled, dreamless sleep.

She awoke to find O'Shea sitting beside her.

"Hello Nessa, I brought the books you ordered, true romance with a bit of bodice-ripping," he mocked.

Rage boiled up inside her and she was about to say they weren't her choice but decided he wasn't worth the bother. It didn't matter what he thought. So she said a formal "Thank you," then continued, "tell your grandfather I'm sorry. I didn't mean to hurt him. Tell him I'm really truly sorry."

"As a matter of fact...."

She could feel the tears gathering and, determined not to cry in front of him again, turned her face to the wall saying, "Please go away...please."

He didn't say anything. But she heard the chair scrape and his footsteps retreating.

A few days later Doctor O'Brien called and looking puzzled said, "You're a bit of an enigma; your fever has gone, your lungs are clear but you're not making progress. Not eating, I hear. Don't you want to get better?"

"I don't really care."

"That's a terrible thing to say, a beautiful young girl like you, privileged, teaching career ahead of you...what's the matter?"

"I don't know...I feel...what's the point? I never felt like this before....always fought back no matter what...but I feel useless and, and...."

"Has O'Shea anything to do with it?"

"Well, sort of...."

"I knew it," he said slapping his knee and going off in a huge guffaw. "Lovesick...give him time, he's fighting it but losing."

"Losing what?"

"The battle...his feeling for you!"

"Oh yeah...his feelings are crystal clear, he hates me and...the only thing I feel for O'Shea is fear. I thought he was going to kill me."

"O'Shea kill you?" O'Brien laughed. "Ah now, Nessa, you were hallucinating, your temperature was sky high...."

"I know I was feverish, but I didn't imagine what I saw, you didn't see his face...the hatred...."

"Why would he hate you?"

"I did a terrible thing...I didn't mean to...I caused his grandfather great sorrow.... I wish I could undo the damage I did to the old man."

"How could you damage Fionn?"

"By being granddaughter of the love of his life.... I went into O'Shea's shop, he had told me not to, and...and the old man was really upset...he thought I was Deirdre...."

"Deirdre?"

"Deirdre, my grandmother, his fiancée...."

"*That* Deirdre.... I know all about her...Fionn's magnificent obsession! And you're her granddaughter, well, well, well...but that's hardly your fault."

"Tell that to O'Shea."

"You probably gave the old man a new lease of life."

"I don't think so...not according to O'Shea."

"I'll see Fionn and sort things out...and I thought you were pining for the young fella, fancied meself as a matchmaker...even asked Owen to bring you the books, thought it would cheer you up...and he was dead keen."

"More wishful thinking on your part...."

"You have to admit he's a fine fella, the nurses here are all ga-ga about him."

"They're welcome to him...before I became really ill I thought I might be...."

"Mmm...?"

"You know, falling for him...anyway, he cured me completely. I have no interest whatsoever in him."

"Getaway."

"Honestly, what frightens me most is my bad judgement. He was so angry, so vicious."

"So he was angry, but be honest he didn't do anything to hurt you now did he?"

"I put out my hand to him and he knocked it away and...."

"He caught you and carried you up to bed, wrapped you in a dry blanket and drove like the clappers to me, hauled me out of a surgery full of patients and had me here faster than the fire brigade. He has an abrasive tongue, but he's the kindest of men. Look at the way he minds the old man. The patience he has with him going on and on about Deirdre. And he's also a very respected man in his business."

"His mood swings are dangerous, he should carry a health warning, in fact you should persuade him to see a psychiatrist."

He laughed. "I'll mention it to him."

"I'm serious."

"Of course you are."

She laughed.

"That's more like it."

"Look, I may have misjudged him slightly but we are a disaster together so forget the matchmaking, we're both better off going our separate ways."

"OK."

"To be honest, what I want most is Kathleen. I wish she was back, I really miss her."

"She'll be back next week, won't she?"

"Yes, I think I'll try and persuade her to come to Australia with me."

"To your uncle?"

"Yes, I've been toying with the idea of going for a while. If Kathleen would come, I'd go like a flash. We were out there a few years ago with Gran and we had a great time. Kathleen loved the sun even more than I did. And she got on great with my uncle Oisín's family."

"That might be a good idea, once you're not running away from anything."

"What would I be running away from?"

"Feelings."

"Doctor O'Brien, I told you, I *almost* fell...luckily I saw his dark side before it was too late."

He looked at her, half grinning.

"Honestly, look, I'll do as you say, eat the food, be a model patient if you tell the old man I didn't mean to upset him. I've already asked O'Shea but just in case...."

"No problem, is that it?"

"No, stop O'Shea visiting."

"OK," he sighed, "but I think you're making a great mistake. You know, of course, he more than likely saved your life."

Nessa buried that information in her heart. The last thing she wanted was to be grateful to O'Shea.

Doctor O'Brien sent a message saying he had

accomplished all tasks and expected her to come on in leaps and bounds. She relaxed knowing she wouldn't be disturbed by O'Shea's presence and began to perk up.

At the end of the week Danny came as well as Sally from the bookshop. Danny got the teaching appointment. Nessa was thrilled until he announced his other good news. Barbara wasn't pregnant after all. In fact, he said, he might take the job for a couple of months, get a bit of experience and then take off for Europe, alone. He said this squeezing Nessa's hand hopefully. Nessa wanted to pulverize him. Another one she didn't want to see again.

Sally was full of beans, telling about the customers who came into the shop. And the regular weirdos. Nessa asked about the professor.

"Up to his usual antics, buying one or two books and hiding one or two under his raincoat as well."

Danny asked how they coped in such a situation.

"It's become sort of a game," Sally said, "we just ask about the one under his raincoat. Although this time he was a bit bolder—'Frisk me,' he said."

"Oh, oh," said Danny.

"'So you want to be frisked?' I said, 'Yes, yes,' he said. 'Step inside,' I said. 'My brother will be with you in a minute.' His face and book dropped in unison, left a tenner on the counter and bolted."

Nessa and Sally took a fit of giggles.

"Another dissatisfied customer," Danny said.

"He'll be back—can't resist our Sal," Nessa said.

Sally went red as a beetroot, then enquired about the marriage status of the hunk who called to the bookshop to tell her about Nessa's plight.

Nessa said she was surprised Doctor O'Brien actually called. She expected him to phone, but agreed he was indeed a dote. She had a feeling he was a bachelor but wasn't sure, she would discreetly find out from the nurses.

Sally said she didn't think he was a doctor. The name of the caller was O'Shea.

Nessa said coldly he was single as far as she knew and had an antique shop in Rathmines. Sally said she'd give it a once over on her way home.

The next day as Nessa sat in the solarium reading one of the novels where the heroine was having her way with the hero, Doctor O'Brien sneaked up on her.

"Don't look now, Nessa, I've a visitor for you, he persuaded me to let him come."

Nessa's heart stopped, then hammered in her chest. Oh God, he's brought O'Shea, I knew he wouldn't give up.

"Stop getting yourself in a state; it's not O'Shea, it's Fionn O'Connor."

She was so glad to see the old man, she flung her arms around him. He held her gently and kissed her softly on the cheek.

"I'll leave ye and love ye," said O'Brien, hurrying off.

"You are looking peaky. We'll have to fatten you up."

"Can't fatten a thoroughbred."

They sat in silence just smiling at each other. Then Nessa said, "I'm sorry I upset you, I didn't mean...."

"Nessa, you've no idea how wonderful it is for

me to find you, painful yes but anything or anyone
to do with Deirdre is precious to me. I would like to
know what happened in that six months that made
her change her mind. I know in my heart she loved
me...you can see it in the picture...those eyes...."

"Yes, the way she's looking at you...so wistful
and full of love."

"Yes, we were so happy together. She was all I
ever wanted."

"I wish I could help you but I don't know
anything...it's so unlike her.... I could write to
Oisín...if anyone knows it'll be him...."

"Would you my dear? It's too late for Deirdre
and me but I would go to my grave happy if I knew
what the circumstances were. Even if they hurt. I
just want to know. When you fall in love, Nessa, go
for it, don't let anything stand in your way.... I
should have demanded her address, sought her
out...found her and taken her away. We were
meant for each other."

Nessa managed to hold the tears in pools, then
feigned a sneeze to wipe her eyes and blow her
nose. Her heart wanted to tell him about Oisín, his
son, but she had no proof. The likeness was almost
certain proof, but what if she was wrong...? She
should confide in O'Shea...but she recoiled at the
thought, no telling how he'd react...make her gran
worse in his eyes.... The doctor, she could discuss it
with him. He'd know what to do, what to say. At
least he'd know what was best for the old man.

She walked to the front door with Fionn. O'Shea
was waiting. They nodded to each other civilly. To
cover their awkwardness and for the sake of the old
man, she asked O'Shea to put a note on the door

telling Kathleen where she was.

O'Shea said he'd do better than that, he'd collect Kathleen at the airport.

She said icily there was no need, the note would do fine.

He bowed. "Whatever the lady wants."

They left, Fionn promising to visit her at home the following week. O'Shea said he'd bring him the following Tuesday.

Kathleen came. Big and blowsy, glowing with a honey tan. Radiant. Kathleen was in love.

Squeezing the life out of Nessa in a bear hug she said, "Oh Nessa you should see him, he's only brilliant," and blushing crimson, "he loves me, well he says he does and he did for the last ten days. I had the happiest ten days of my life."

Oh God, thought Nessa, she's fallen for one of those gorgeous Italian fellas who break the hearts of gullible tourists.

Seeing Nessa's face Kathleen continued, "He's not like that, not one of those gigolos or beach bums, or whatever you call them. Mario is different. I don't care what anyone thinks. I love him and I'll love him till the day I die. Oh Nessa, if you met him you'd feel the same."

Nessa felt glad and sad for Kathleen. At this moment in time she radiated happiness but her heart was bound to be broken by that beach romeo.

Nessa sighed.

"And what about you?"

Nessa told her about O'Shea and the old man, leaving out the horrible bits O'Shea said about her grandmother, because from the time Gran took

Kathleen under her wing she was completely devoted to Deirdre. If she knew what he said she'd go after him, might even knife him.

"He's a fine thing though...if I wasn't so madly in love with Mario...."

"Sorry...who's a fine thing?"

"Owen...."

"How do you know?"

"When he met me at the airport...."

"He met...?"

"Didn't you send him?"

"Well no, not exactly...we had a bit of a row...in fact a bloody great one....and.... Wait a minute how did he know....?"

"He held up this big card with KATHLEEN—FRIEND OF NESSA'S written in huge letters...I had to laugh."

"Hilarious," Nessa said.

"Just as well he did come, I'd have been stranded, hadn't a bean...not even the bus-fare."

Nessa squirmed; she had forgotten she had arranged to pick Kathleen up and, being so busy standing on her dignity, was prepared to sacrifice poor Kathleen. She couldn't believe she could be so self-centred. Thank God O'Shea ignored her.

"Did he mention me?"

"Yes, said he had some clothes belonging to you."

"Clothes...what clothes?"

"A bra and a blouse, said you left them in his car." She hooted with laughter.

"You don't understand. I can explain."

"I'm all ears, he also took a sweater from your flat, said he lent it to you when you stripped in his jeep. I think you should tell me your story again—this time the unexpurgated edition."

Furious, Nessa told about the punctures, everything, but still excluding his remarks about Deirdre, although this time she was sorely tempted to prove to Kathleen what a brute he was.

The next day, Kathleen collected her from the hospital in Nessa's car and brought her home.

"See you got the puncture mended, thanks."

"What puncture?" Kathleen said.

"The front wheel, I remember the air hissing out of it as I bashed it against the kerb."

"Maybe O'Shea fixed it when he brought your underwear back." Kathleen laughed and laughed.

Nessa had a score to settle with that bastard O'Shea.

CHAPTER FOUR

Putting the key in the door Nessa said, "Did you hang up my suit?"

"Yes, yes, everything is in its place."

"That'd be a miracle."

And it was a miracle. Everything was in its place, and clean. Windows gleaming, curtains washed, books dusted, table set, a delicious smell of dinner cooking. Nessa hugged Kathleen.

"Oh Kay, you're so good to me."

Kathleen shuffled, embarrassed.

"I'm not, I didn't.... Owen did it, or had it done. Sent a team in. I could have stopped him, but I thought it needed a good scrub."

"Thanks."

"Well, you're not exactly house-proud."

"You're right and you did the right thing, I'll send him a thank you note. I owe him one already."

"Good," said Kathleen beaming. "I made the casserole myself."

After the meal, Kathleen went to her own flat and Nessa wrote to O'Shea:

Dear Mr O'Shea,

Thank you for making my flat respectable. I have decided to mend my slovenly ways. Thank you also for returning my clothes. I would rather you had given them to me personally or at least discreetly wrapped when you gave them to Kathleen. She has the complete wrong end of the stick concerning them. Doesn't believe my version. If you should ever see her again, please verify my account.

Doctor O'Brien tells me you probably saved my life. Sorry for being so ungracious about it. But I didn't want to know. You see, every time I drifted into sleep, you had me pinned against the wall, your face full of hatred, and I'd wake in a pool of sweat, terrified. Which is ironic really, because when you arrived that morning, I was so thankful. I thought you were my knight in shining armour come to rescue me. It never occurred to me you were more into doing me an injury than saving me. I was so thick, I didn't realise I'd done anything wrong, apart, of course, from being a nosy bitch. Your grandfather and I had got on so well.

I have a bit of a dilemma. I told Fionn I'd write to my uncle in Australia and see if he knew the circumstances of your grandfather's alleged betrayal by my grandmother. On reflection maybe it would not be a good idea. I don't want to cause any more grief to anyone, especially my uncle, who is very precious to me.

What do you think?

Write don't call. I may not hear the bell.

Thanks again for saving my life and cleaning my hovel.

Yours gratefully,
Nessa Walsh.

She put it in an envelope and posted it.
He replied by return of post:

Dear Ms Walsh,
   Thank you for your letter, you have no need to be grateful to me. I behaved abominably. I feel only shame and can't excuse my behaviour. If I'd listened to Fionn properly, I wouldn't have done what I did, I'm only glad some good came out of it, ie, that I was able to get O'Brien for you. Had I not come the postman would have done as much, only without verbally abusing you first.
   I hope your nightmares are gone for good. I had no intention of harming you.
   About the other matter. I really don't know the answer. Maybe wait a while. I don't think Fionn could take it (in spite of what he says) if, and quite probably when, your uncle proves Deirdre was not the sweet trusting soul "got at" by person or persons unknown and made marry a well-to-do doctor.
Sweet dreams,
Owen O'Shea.

The bastard, Nessa thought, always a sting or a barb. Has to make an innuendo about Gran.

   More than ever, she wanted to clear her grandmother's name. Prove she was good. Rub O'Shea's nose in it. She knew Gran wouldn't deliberately hurt anyone. There had to be some explanation.

   Maybe she'd write to her uncle and tell him about meeting an old man who painted a portrait of Gran and claimed to be her fiancé. If he knew anything and wanted to pursue it he could. At least it would be Oisín's decision. She couldn't help thinking she was stirring up a hornet's nest.

Fionn appeared as arranged on Tuesday afternoon, looking like an old military gentleman from his trimmed moustache to his shoes polished like new chestnuts and his silver-topped walking stick. He brought flowers. Carnations.

To stop him pumping her about Deirdre and Oisín, Nessa asked about his daughter and Owen.

"Well," Fionn said, "Connie and I had only the one child, Maureen. Born in nineteen-forty-two in London, Ontario. When she was five we moved to London, England. We both would have liked more children but when none came we just accepted the fact. Maureen, being the only one, was very precious. Completely doted on by both of us. Whatever Maureen wanted, Maureen got. She got a bit wild in her teens, a child of her time...into Elvis in a big way, with her DA haircut and her long skinny shirt and teddy boyfriends, literally with blue suede shoes and drainpipe trousers."

"My mother was an Elvis fan too, and that fellow who was killed in the plane crash...Buddy Holly. Gran kept her scrap books and her photo album for me. Herself and her friends were into these full skirts with all the petticoats. They looked like cabbages. Gran said they used to stick kiss-curls to their cheeks with soap, and one of Mam's friends stiffened her petticoat with sugar going to a dance."

"Bet she came to a sticky end," Fionn laughed.

"Apparently, she did. Gran said it melted in the heated ballroom." Nessa grinned. "Mam had

Beatle records too, but the King was her idol."

"By the time The Beatles were on the scene, Maureen was well and truly married."

"Married?"

"Yes, at the tender age of eighteen, just after her A-levels, Maureen met Owen O'Shea, a pacifist, and married him."

"You allowed her marry at eighteen?" Nessa said incredulous.

"We were reeling in shock, blaming ourselves for giving her her head. At first we thought he was another of her fads, so different. We could have stopped her marrying him, she was under twenty-one but we didn't want to alienate her. She was besotted and would have gone off with him anyway, so we gave them our blessing. As it turned out it was the right thing."

"They were happy?"

"Yes, very. He was a twenty-seven year old anthropologist and an avid ban-the-bomb marcher. A lovely fellow, and kind. Into saving the earth when nobody cared."

"What year was that?"

"Nineteen-sixty."

"That's the year my mother met my father, they didn't marry till sixty-two," Nessa said.

"Owen was born nine months later, April sixty-one...."

"Bet that changed her lifestyle."

"Not a bit of it. Owen was hauled around the world on their backs. We offered to mind him, but they wouldn't hear of it. They turned up every so often and sometimes stayed for months. When hemlines swept the floor, like all good flower

people they headed for San Francisco, literally
with flowers in their hair."

"And Owen?"

"With them, of course. Connie used to say his
umbilical cord was woven in daisy chains. They
loved him very much, and in a very unorthodox
way he had a good early childhood and education.
They settled in Italy for about five years. Maureen
changed her name to Magda and began to paint
while Owen dug up the past. Magda never came
out of that phase, still a beatnik. Albeit an aging
one. Eventually when Owen was ten they came
to live in Wicklow."

"Why Ireland?"

"Both Owen's parents were Irish and he had
spent his childhood there. And Maureen of course
was half-Irish. Also Ireland still had virgin soil
and Owen wanted to grow vegetables organically.
Owen and Maureen, uninterested in material
things and scorned capitalists, accepted handouts
from *this* capitalist," Fionn laughed. "They let me
buy them the house. I did it for Owen junior, put
it in his name, hoping they'd set down roots."

"And did they?"

"Sort of...if the house was in their name they
probably would have sold it and gone away sooner.
As it was they stayed for a few years and then for
a few months each year."

"And how did Owen junior get on in Wicklow?"

"Caused quite a stir in the village school with
his shoulder length hair and tie-dyed shirts. Not
to mention his beatnik parents."

"I can imagine."

"When the teacher asked him what he knew

about Heaven and Hell, Owen said, 'Dad says Hell hath no fury like a woman scorned, when Magda is throwing a tantrum and whatever else she can lay her hands on.' And when the teacher asked about Heaven, he sang a few bars of a song called *Dancing Cheek To Cheek*..... It goes something like this...'I'm in heaven and my heart beats so that I can hardly speak.... '"

"What did the teacher say?"

"She was amused, a young teacher, only out of training college."

"Was Owen upset, did the other kids jeer him?"

"Not at all, they thought he was a hero. Someone who could make the teacher laugh and wasn't afraid of Hell. He took to the place like a duck to water. Maureen remained restless, always wanting to take off. 'Can't cage a wild bird,' Owen used to say, 'it would destroy her.' So they wandered at least a few months of the year, sometimes longer. Joined digs all over the world. They gave young Owen an awesome freedom, no strings attached, no hassle, no pressure, any dream, any aspiration, accepted."

"Sounds idyllic."

"Not really, he was inhibited by too much freedom. No walls to break out of. When other teenagers were defying their parents, he was trying to break into society. Because it didn't matter whether he did well or not at school, he pushed himself. Glowing reports, perfect behaviour, brought bewilderment to his parents. All Magda said when he brought home the prizes was, 'If that's what turns you on, love.' What he wanted was real parents. Morning and night prayers, a bit of nagging. A solid framework to rail against.

"When he was a teenager he spent more and more time with us, much to our delight, while they sowed their wild oats. Unfortunately they never stopped sowing them. Eventually Owen lived with us in Essex and holidayed with them. It was an ideal arangement. Connie and I wallowed in his achievements and Owen was a happy, studious lad."

Nessa almost felt sorry for O'Shea. At least for the teenage O'Shea.

"Maureen...Magda, she's much more a Magda than a Maureen...was full of affection as well as affectation. She loves Owen senior and junior and me passionately, but a bit carelessly."

"She sounds an intriguing character."

"She's that all right, also very self-centred. I benefit from her fecklessness. She treats me like a normal, rational human being, even a contemporary, no fussing. Even brought me to the West with her last year on a painting expedition. Bullied me into painting too. First time in fifty years. It was exhilarating. We painted in the daytime and pub-crawled at night. The craic was mighty as they say. Unfortunately I got a cold but it was well worth it. Owen was furious. They had a terrible row, turned into to a slagging match. He accused her of carelessness and told her she was no longer a flower person, she'd long gone to seed. She said she never thought she'd produce such a stuffy weed and to think she called him the light of her life.... At least she embraced life. 'On whose backs?' he shouted, launching into a few home truths, calling her selfish and greedy and having a me-first-the-rest-after mentality. I think it was the only time she saw herself as others see her.

"She became good and caring for about a week. It was a terrible strain. Even Owen was relieved when she reverted. They compromised, she promised to be a bit more responsible, and he to loosen up and be less protective of me. After a week they were exactly as they were before."

"Is she still painting?"

"Yes, and quite good. When she began she copied others, now she has developed her own style. I'm surprised just how good she is and is being recognised. Selling a few pictures here and there for tidy sums and being careful with it... almost miserly."

"As a result of the row with Owen?"

"No, I wouldn't say so, more probably because it's her own. Could end up rich, or at least comfortable. I don't mind telling you that in itself is a great relief."

"And her husband?"

"He's in the Amazon. Joined up with some Indian tribe to save the rain-forest. Actually, I think he did this solo trip to get away from her for a while. She's very wearing. They now have a sort of open marriage according to Magda. They'll more than likely end up together. They write regularly. There isn't anyone else in their lives, well no one permanent. Magda may have the odd toy-boy of course."

"Of course," said Nessa, gobsmacked.

"I'd better make a move, don't want to

overstay...I've been warned."

"Doctor O'Brien?"

"No, Owen." She was about to say he should mind his own business, when Fionn continued, "Said I mustn't tire you."

"That's very considerate of him." She almost meant it.

"He's that sort of person."

Nessa linked Fionn out into the hallway. A note lay on the mat:

"Ms Walsh, chauffeur outside. Afraid to ring bell. Owen."

They found O'Shea asleep in the car, the window down.

Vulnerable, Nessa thought, as she looked in on the sleeping O'Shea. No he isn't. I'm just suffering Fionn's brainwashing, well, his good PR job.... She may have felt a little sorry for the teenage O'Shea but it wasn't going to affect her feelings for this full-grown version.

While she gently nuzzled him with one hand she pinched him hard with the other. He jumped, literally hitting the roof.

Fionn chortled. O'Shea was peeved.

"Sorry," Nessa whispered full of contrition. "I didn't mean...."

He shot her a withering glance.

"Ah, Owen, be fair, you can't blame Nessa, she barely touched you."

"Sometimes that's all it takes. I dreamt I was being pinched by a poisonous spider."

"If you could bottle that, Nessa, a touch that sends men crashing through the ceiling."

"And call it The Touch of the Spider Woman,"

Nessa said.

Fionn and Nessa fell about laughing. O'Shea didn't even smile.

A few days passed and Kathleen had sunk into despondency.

"Nothing from Mario," Kathleen said, her eyes brimming.

"Relax Kay, he wouldn't have gotten your letter yet."

"I sent it Swiftpost."

"Still, it's only six days. He couldn't possibly get it and reply yet. I only got your card on Monday."

"I suppose.... Anyway, even if it was only a holiday romance on his part, it was worth it. I'm glad it happened," she said defiantly.

"You look washed out—do yourself up."

"For what?"

"We could go out for a drive and a drink. Thought we'd make the most of the car while we have it, you know the insurance is up at the end of the month and I'll be selling it...."

"I don't feel like it."

"Ah go on, I haven't been out for weeks and I feel bloody awful too."

"God, Nessa," said Kathleen, jumping up, "of course we'll go. I'll just shower and wash my hair."

"Thanks," said Nessa, "I'll come back in half an hour."

"I'll be ready."

It was a lovely summer evening. Nessa sat watching the swallows dive and dart around the garden. It seemed so long since she had sat there getting ready for the auction. Only three weeks. So many things had happened; Kathleen whirled around in the fast lane for two weeks and she had her own little drama. Now everything had slowed down, like they were nudged into a siding.

She thought about Australia. She wanted to get away. O'Shea kept creeping into her thoughts and while she didn't like him she was dangerously attracted to him. Even after terrifying her. Should she believe him when he said he'd never harm her? Maybe all men who beat up women say that. Anyway, it was irrelevant now. The chances of her being in a situation where she might find out were remote.

Probably when Kathleen realises it was only a holiday affair, she might be glad to go to Australia with her. She would broach the subject over a drink. Then play it by ear.

She locked up and went down.

"My God, there's a transformation, last time I saw you you looked like an aul one," Nessa said laughing.

"Thanks very much, I felt like one too."

The bell rang.

Nessa's heart stopped. O'Shea....

"Will you get it, Nessa, while I go to the loo?"

Nessa went reluctantly and opened the hall door. A huge bunch of red roses were thrust at her, followed by a mass of black curls and smiling, almost black, eyes. The smile turned to disappointment when he discovered Nessa.

"Mario?"

He nodded.

"Nessa," pointing to herself. "Kathleen's in

there."

She put her finger to her lips. Then shouted to Kathleen, "I've forgotten my bag, you go on out to the car, won't be a minute."

She raced up the stairs as screams and gasps of joy emanated from below. She looked over the banister to see Mario being devoured by Kathleen.

Nessa crept in to her flat as great wafts of sadness swept over her.... She wanted to feel what Kathleen was feeling right now. Delirious, delicious happiness. She felt lonelier than she ever felt in her entire life.

Her budding passion for O'Shea. That day at the school. Going home so ill, yet bolstered by his smile. Only lasting half a day. She sighed. Ah well...lust, that's probably what she felt for O'Shea, pure unadultered lust. Kept getting flashes of him naked. She blamed her fever. Anyway, the only passion he showed for her was when he pinned her against the wall in hate.

And now she might be losing Kathleen. Mario seemed as besotted as her.

Kathleen knocked timidly on her door. "Nessa, I want you to meet someone."

The two of them stood holding hands in the doorway, radiating such happiness the place glowed. Kathleen said she wanted to show Mario off and both herself and Mario insisted she come out with them for a drink at least. Nessa assented, knowing in her heart she should have refused. Why was she always doing this, saying yes when she meant no?

Mario had hired a snazzy car and they drove to Howth. They walked along the pier watching the fishermen landing their catch, then went up to The Abbey Tavern for a drink.

Nessa felt like the greatest gooseberry in the world. To escape, and to give them a chance to gaze at each other without having to consider her, Nessa went into the ladies and sat there as long as she could. Coming out she saw O'Shea and a lovely blonde girl chatting to Kathleen and Mario. Nessa stayed in the shadows. She recognised the girl from somewhere but couldn't place her. The girl excused herself, kissed O'Shea on the lips and began moving away.

"Susan," he called, catching her hand and left with her in spite of her laughing protests. On the cover of glossies, Nessa remembered. The girl was a model.

As soon as they were out of sight, Nessa went over to the table and sat down. Kathleen leaned forward excitedly. Before she could say a word, O'Shea came up behind Nessa and whispered in her ear.

"Of all the gin joints in all the world, you happen to come into my local."

Nessa swung round. "Don't play it again Sam, I couldn't bear it."

"Bogey never said...."

"I know, I know, I was being sarcastic. I hate misquotes."

"I didn't know I was in the presence of a movie buff."

"You're not, I am just sick to death with halfwits being *original* with bogus Bogey quotes. It seems to be a family trait, your grandfather is into it too."

"OhmyGod,hereditary...probably incurable... the sins of the grandfather visited on his grandson. Is that a correct quote, Ms Walsh?"

"In your case it has to be, as misquotes are your legacy."

"Well thank you, Ms Walsh, for making exceptions for us poor ignorant folk."

Mario was looking from one to the other, lost. His English was very good but he couldn't keep up with this banter.

O'Shea, seeing Mario's plight, spoke to him in perfect Italian. Mario laughed and replied. O'Shea laughed.

"What did he say?" Kathleen asked O'Shea.

"Ad verbatim, 'Love is a many splendoured thing.'"

Nessa and Kathleen cracked up laughing, visibly lightening the scene. "You live around here?" Nessa asked.

"Up the hill, I thought you'd come to seek me out. Have a snoop around my place."

She looked down at the table-mat and said nothing.

"I have asked these good people to dine with me at my place and they have graciously accepted. I hope you'll do the same."

Nessa was about to say she had a previous engagement when O'Shea said, "I hope you won't suddenly remember a previous appointment, Nessa."

Nessa didn't answer.

"I'll fix you up with a partner."

"Oh goody, so I won't have to go out in the highways and byways and snare some poor innocent and make him accompany me to the feast?"

"Got it in one, I couldn't bear having to throw him out if he wasn't suitably attired."

"Thanks, but no thanks...I really do have a previous appointment."

"I haven't said which day."

"Actually, I'm busy all week."

"Fionn will be there and you've been neglecting him lately...he's beginning to fret. You'll be Fionn's date."

"I'm sorry, really...."

Kathleen gave her an I'm-not-going-if-you're-not look, accompanied by a kick on the shin.

She capitulated. "When?"

"Tomorrow night, eight."

"If I can cancel my appointment."

"You really have one?"

"Yes," she lied. "Strange as it may seem, I do get the odd invitation from eligible young men, sometimes I'm not even grateful and I refuse."

"So you will be Fionn's date," he laughed.

"I'd like that. We have a lot in common. We like the same things. The same—"

He interrupted, "Quotations."

Ignoring him, she continued, "—the same people. I was terrified you'd try and fix me up with someone from the getting-desperate-age-group, you know, that thirty-something pathetic shower."

"Nessa!" Kathleen said, horrified.

"Oh I'm sorry Mr O'Shea, I didn't mean to be rude about your age."

"Didn't you, Ms Walsh?" His eyes twinkled.

She wanted to tear his clothes off.

"Why not come up now and see my etchings?"

"I...I...."

"Excuse me," he said to Kathleen and Mario, taking Nessa aside.

"Don't you know three is a crowd?"

"Of course I bloody well know. You don't think I want to be here. I've spent most of the evening in the loo trying to keep out of their way. They insisted I come. I want to get out of here more than anything else in the world but I don't want to let them know I feel shut out."

"I'll take you home."

"Thank you."

Turning to Mario and Kathleen, O'Shea said, "Nessa has declined my invitation to come up and see my etchings, instead she has suggested we watch the moon coming up over the bay. Hope you don't mind me taking her away?"

Kathleen, with mouth hanging open, shook her head.

"See you tomorrow at eight. Here's my address," Owen said, shaking hands with both and handing Mario his card.

Nessa waved and smiled. Mario and Kathleen beamed a you-too smile at her.

As they reached the seafront, Nessa stopped and leaned against the bus stop saying, "Thanks for getting me out of that mortifying situation."

"No problem. You shouldn't have gotten yourself into it in the first place, have you no savvy?"

"Not a lot."

"Anyone could see they needed to be alone."

"Even me, but then I'm really into gooseberrying

in a big way."

"So it seems."

"My grandmother never told me about gooseberrying, probably thought I'd have enough cop on not to stay where I wasn't wanted. Thank you for helping me mend my selfish ways."

"Glad to be of service, probably not your fault, it seems to be a nasty family trait. Hope it's curable."

"Oooh, you really know how to hurt me, I knew the evening wouldn't pass without a snipe at my grandmother."

"I'm sorry."

"You don't really think I'd deliberately set out to spoil Kathleen and Mario's evening. I only went along because they insisted. I didn't want to go. But I didn't want to hurt my very best friend who didn't want to exclude me from her happiness. It wasn't a good idea but it was done with the best of intentions on both our parts."

"You should learn to say no. Shouldn't let people talk you into doing things you don't want to, then expect others to rescue you whinging from your dilemma."

"I don't expect you to come to my rescue—I'm not Lois Lane and you're definitely not Superman."

"Not quite, but you were glad of my help or were you lying just now?"

"Of course I was glad. Didn't I thank you for your wonderful feat?"

"You did."

"And you're right, dead right, I am a cringing eejit. From now on I'll say no and mean it and I'll put it in practice right now."

"Good."

"I don't want to go to your old dinner party. You only want me there to ridicule me...tease me...make me a laughing stock."

"Would I do such a thing?"

"Yes you bloody well would, so you can get into your jeep and fuck off into the sunset and leave me alone. I'm getting the bus home."

"Suit yourself, you silver-tongued little charmer," he said, walking away.

Is biting your nose to spite your face yet another family failing, Nessa mused as she stood waiting for ages for the bus. She conceded it probably was. And her grandmother would be most dissappointed with her using gutter language. She was ashamed of herself.

Walking up tree-lined Griffith Avenue she felt nervous. Pools of darkness spread around the sturdy tree trunks. She expected a rapist or mugger to leap out of the dark and attack her. She walked on the edge of the path. After a while she was aware of a car kerb-crawling behind her.

Don't panic, don't look around, behave nonchalantly, she told herself. And be prepared...kick him, gouge his eyes and knee him in the goolies.... If only she'd walked on the far side of the road facing the traffic she'd be much safer. Ahead, the traffic lights were red. As she arrived at them, she dashed across the road, aware of the car but not looking at it.... She felt a bit safer. The car was still stalking her. Crawling. At least now there was the width of the road between them.... Kick him, gouge his eyes and knee him, she repeated like a mantra.

She could see her house. Even with her key in her hand she wouldn't have enough time to get in and keep him out. Approaching her house, she decided her best strategy was to walk on a few hundred yards, go around the corner, then leg it home. She'd be safely in before he could turn the car and come back. He wouldn't even know which house.

She went around the corner, then doubled back and raced up the road on cotton-wool legs. Outside her house, tucked in behind her own car, the black car waited. A man in black barred her way.

Motionless, she stood. Her practised ear-splitting roar stuck her throat. Her hands flew up, shivering violently.

The man spoke. "A pushover, literally rooted to the spot in fear."

She didn't respond.

He shook her gently, "Nessa, it's me, Owen...you know, O'Shea, the one you told to fuck off into the sunset?"

O'Shea, it's O'Shea, only O'Shea...her mind began to function.

She clung to him. "I'm so glad.... A man in a car followed me...."

She looked at the black car and pointed, "That's the car...."

"It's mine, I was that man...."

"You?" she said incredulously.

"I followed the bus, then you, worried about you walking home alone."

"So you crawled along behind me, scaring me half to death. Why didn't you call out to me?"

"I knew you were aware of the car, thought you knew it was me, with your head held snottily erect."

"Did you not see me trying to whistle a happy tune? Anyway, where's your jeep?"

"I use that for work, this for play."

"It's very small."

"It's a sports model."

"I can see that, I'm not stupid."

"Steady, flatten down the hackles."

She ran her hands down her body.

"There, all flattened," she laughed. "I am grateful, it was really kind of you escorting me home, especially..." she paused embarrassed, "after what I said."

He looked at her, almost smiling.

"Come up for coffee?"

"Better not, best leave on a high note. Still friendly."

"Tell your grandfather I'll call to see him tomorrow."

"He won't be there. I thought it would be best if he rested tomorrow, ready for a late night."

"Well, the next day."

"Actually, he's going home to Wicklow the day after tomorrow. He won't be in Dublin for a while. I'm going abroad for a month."

"What about your business?"

"I always close for the month of July, combine a bit of collecting around Europe with a holiday."

"I see, I may be going away myself."

"Really, where?"

"Australia.... Thinking of emigrating."

"Why?"

"Nothing here for me, no real job. Kathleen will follow Mario to the ends of the earth, well Sardinia anyway, if he asks her. And it looks like he will. So I'll go to Australia, be near my remaining family; uncle, aunt and cousins."

"You didn't get the teaching post."

"Danny got it, undeservedly as it so happens."

"Tut-tut, sour grapes."

"It's no such thing; at first I was thrilled, really delighted. But when he told me he was only going to take it for a few months then head off to Europe I was furious."

"You might get it when he goes."

"No chance, I told them I wasn't interested."

"I don't understand, you wanted this job and when you went for the interview—"

Nessa interrupted, "Look, Danny told me at the second interview his girlfriend was pregnant and he needed the job desperately. I felt sorry for them, so I did what I had to do, then he comes to see me in hospital telling me he got it, Barbara wasn't pregnant, they were splitting up and he was thinking of going to Spain solo and would I come with him. The cheek of the bast...."

She stopped. O'Shea was grinning at her.

"I'd better go."

"Enjoy your trip."

"Thanks, goodnight Nessa, sweet dreams."

Oh God I think I love him.... Susan, remember Susan...his girlfriend Susan *and* his mood swings; nice now, nasty next, nice nasty, nice nasty.... I want to kiss his beautiful mouth...feel his warm body next to mine...my last chance...might never see him again.... Kathleen would jump him there and then...she wanted to do just that....

"Tell your grandfather I was asking for him," she said out loud.

"Will do, expect we'll see you before you go...."

"I'm not sure...it depends on my visa; if it comes through quickly I might be gone by the end of July."

She wanted to throw him on his back and have her way with him.

What am I thinking, what's got into me? Is my face betraying me?

"You could come tomorrow night in that case...."

"Am I still invited?"

"Only if you want to."

"I'd love to."

"Good," he said, kissing her softly and tenderly on the lips. She kissed him back, pressing her body against him. He kissed her again.

"Goodnight, Nessa. See you tomorrow."

She didn't want him to go. Tomorrow she'd have to share him with Susan.

"Coffee?" she said

"Better leave while I'm winning, don't want to jeopardise tomorrow night, see ya."

"Bye, Owen."

He walked to his car.

Hanging on to the magic moment she followed him, calling, "Do you think I should take my own car or go with Kathleen and Mario?"

"Come with them, you can't do too much gooseberrying on a fifteen minute drive."

"I was thinking more of the journey home—say they wanted to moon gaze or something?"

"I'll leave you home. Or drive behind you if we have a row."

"Hardly another row so soon, I'll be on my very best behaviour."

"Me too."

She kissed him again.

"Goodnight, Nessa," he said.

She dreamt about Owen O'Shea all night.

CHAPTER FIVE

The day burst on Nessa with sunshine glaring through the light curtains making her squint.

O'Shea was on her mind. She could only think of O'Shea's lips brushing hers. She snuggled into the duvet. The house was creaking awake. Pipes tingling, floor boards expanding in the sunlight. She heard a light giggle. Followed by a deep barrel laugh. Imagine if it was me and O'Shea? The improbability of it made it more exciting. A coup. To woo him, make him desire her. Is that what she wanted?

She wanted him to want her as herself, warts and all.

Today she'd keep out of the lovers' way. Not even go with them to Howth. Tell them she'd meet them there. So they wouldn't have to consider her in their plans.

Wide awake panic...what to wear? She rummaged through her wardrobe. God I've nothing, not a screed...the black one I wore to the Trinity ball.... Too posh. Nothing else. She'd buy something plain but chic. The dinner wouldn't be formal or anything, not at a day's notice. Probably a fairly casual affair. Susan would probably be designerishly casual. Susan's name caused a little barb to scratch her heart, bringing her back to reality. Susan and Owen, Susan and Owen, she repeated killing the fantasy. Well almost.

She still wanted to give it her best shot but didn't want to fork out on something she might never wear again. Something plain that she could dickey up. She had loads of costume jewellery and she had to count her pennies. She'd go in to town early, get a dress, call in to Sally at the bookshop and ask her if her brother was still interested in the car, maybe give in her notice. No, better not yet. She wasn't as sure about Australia today as she was yesterday. Maybe if she hung around for the rest of the summer, herself and O'Shea might get together. Susan, she half-heartedly reminded herself, but O'Shea without Susan filled her mind. She'd put her name down in a few TEFL places. With a bit of luck she'd get July and August teaching English to foreign students.

She knocked on Kathleen's door. Kathleen, dewy-eyed, answered. Nessa told her she'd meet herself and Mario in Howth as she wasn't sure of her plans. Kathleen said they'd probably go for a spin to Wicklow and maybe do a little shopping.

Sitting in a traffic jam on the quays, Nessa hummed...imagining him.... Never before had she realised Dublin was so beautiful or the sky so like candy floss.

She tried on dress after dress, they all seemed to make her look like a tart or a kid.

She went to the bookshop. Sally said she was delighted to see her, but she clearly wasn't. Something on her mind.

"Spit it out, Sal," Nessa said.

So Sally did.

She wouldn't need Nessa anymore on a Saturday. Couldn't afford her. Nessa assured her she didn't mind even though she did. She said she understood perfectly and was grateful to her for keeping her on so long. Sally, relieved, made them both a cup of coffee. Said she noticed O'Shea driving by slowly, looking in, and last Saturday he came in and bought some books.

"Did he now?" said Nessa, hoping he was looking for her. The hopeful look on Sally's face said she too had the same wish. She rang her brother and he said if Nessa brought the car around right away he'd have a look at it.

Nessa drove to Rathmines. Dermot, small and round like Sally, examined it minutely. He offered her one thousand five hundred pounds. Nessa laughed derisively. Two thousand five hundred, only one careful female driver...and only two years old...well...almost three.

Dermot said he'd give her two thousand cash if she gave it to him there and then. Nessa agreed if he'd drive her into the city. The deal was done and Nessa was rich.

Everything was coming to an end, Nessa realised. The lease on the flat would be up this year, too. Gran had bought the car for her twentieth birthday, when she rented the flats for them. One house, two separate flats, she had insisted, so Nessa could study and they could form separate friendships and still have each other. They did all that and eventually became each other's best friend.

Having lodged most of the money, she had coffee and a sandwich and went looking in earnest for a dress. She fell in love with a Thirties number in Jenny Vander's. It came to her knees in a swish of silk. She bought a silver beaded bag to go with it and a pair of Thirties leather silver shoes in Mother Redcap's market for a fiver. A long cigarette holder would complete the picture, she thought. Then dismissed the idea.

"Lir" hand-made chocolates and flowers, white flowers, maybe lilies and roses...yes, that's what she'd bring. If she ordered them from the florist at Sutton Cross she could collect them on the way. She bought the chocolates, rang the florist, ordered the flowers and went home totally satisfied.

Her hair...what would she do with it? After her shower it looked like a tangled bush. She ran around to Pam, the hairdresser, who had put her hair up in tiny plaits when she was going for her first interview. Pam pulled and tugged at Nessa's hair, holding it this way and that through half-closed eyes when Nessa asked for a Thirties style. Eventually after much rummaging through books, they decided on finger waving brought down into pin curls. Nessa and Pam were chuffed with the result. On her way home, Nessa ordered a taxi for seven-thirty.

At Sutton Cross the taxi driver gave a little beep. The florist appeared from Cascade Flowers carrying an exquisite bouquet of white roses and lilies with bear grass.

Longi Florium...Longi Florium...Nessa repeated as they drove towards Howth. That's what the

florist said the lilies were called when Nessa asked.
She felt very posh sitting in the taxi surrounded by
goodies....

O'Shea's house was at the end of a long driveway,
smothered in ivy and looking as if it had evolved
from the landscape.

O'Shea opened the door to her. He was dressed
in a white shirt with a coloured silk tie loosely
knotted, black silk jacket and black trousers. She
couldn't check the glow in in her heart and reckoned
it shone through her eyes.

"Don't wear your heart on your sleeve, Nessa,"
her grandfather used to say whȷen she was moping
around as a teenager, madly in love with some
spotty youth or other, "keep them guessing."

O'Shea guessed all right.

He smiled at her, brushing her lips with his.

"You look as if you stepped out of *The Great
Gatsby*."

"Do you like it...?"she twirled.

"I love it, just hope Fionn does, you look more
like your grandmother than your grandmother
herself."

OhmyGod, what a blunder. Fionn and Deirdre's
era. How could I be so dumb?

Chastened, she allowed O'Shea to take her elbow
and steer her into the drawing-room. Fionn stood
up, creaking. He held her two hands. "My dear you
look wonderful, like Ginger Rogers," he said hugging
her. "Doesn't she look divine, Owen?"

She looked at O'Shea, hoping for approval. He
was smiling. "She most certainly does."

Thanks be to God, thought Nessa.

Mario kissed her on both cheeks and Kathleen

squeezed her hand and said, "Howya?"

"Susan?" she asked

"Paris," he said. "I am to play gooseberry unless Fionn agrees to share you with me."

Fionn said it was out of the question.

The room was fine and gracious, overlooking the sea, exquisitely furnished with antiques. It reminded her a bit of her own home, the high ceilings and beautiful furniture, when her grandfather was alive.... He was a collector of beautiful things, especially clocks. Gran sold them off, bit by bit, to fund her waifs and strays.

After drinks and a little small talk they went in to the dining-room. It was totally modern, furnished with chic Alfrank Pompei dining-room suite, lamps, candle sticks, side-tables in grey. And modern Irish paintings on the walls. Dinner was served by O'Shea, probably cooked by gourmet chefs who take over the kitchen and do everything, Nessa decided. Only vaguely aware of what she was eating, Nessa couldn't take her eyes off O'Shea. Everything gelled. They talked about Italian art, all three men were well versed and Nessa knew as much as any of them.

As a child, her grandfather had played spot-the-painter quiz games with her, leaving her with a great love and interest in paintings. He had brought her to Italy a few times to see the great Italian artists.

Kathleen, who also knew her stuff, just listened, gazing at Mario, bursting with pride like a mother whose child had won a gold medal at the feis, as he argued and discussed great works. The evening was magic. Good food, wine and the conversation rivetting. Fionn was so alive, so knowledgeable. He looked younger and kept patting Nessa's hand, beaming. And O'Shea. O'Shea was magnificent. She didn't want the evening to end.

O'Shea suggested they adjourn to the conservatory as the dining-room was chilling slightly. The conservatory was bathed in light and warmth, still holding the heat of the day. Fionn went to the bathroom.

As Nessa sat on a wicker chair her eye caught a writing box on the side-table. It was identical to her own. She ran her fingers over the beautiful old wood, lovingly.

O'Shea's hand came down on hers enveloping and squeezing it, then roughly pushed it off the box.

"Don't."

"What?"

"Don't spoil the evening."

"I have one...I was just...."

"Don't just anything," he said through his teeth, snuffing out her glow. Sadness, almost unbearable sadness, shivered through her. She wanted to howl to the moon in her unhappiness. Please God, don't let it show for the sake of the old man and Kathleen and Mario. But mostly don't let O'Shea see what he can do to me.

As Fionn entered the conservatory, Nessa left for the bathroom. She waited a long time, composing herself. She'd talk to Fionn without showing sadness. She'd make herself, force herself, to look happy, not let that...that.... She couldn't even muster up anger for him.

She returned to the conservatory, carefully

avoiding O'Shea's eyes. He continued to be the charming host, regaling his guests with an amusing anecdote.

"Sit here beside me, Nessa," said Fionn, absently stroking the writing box on the table beside him. Nessa crossed over gratefully, a pasted smile aching her jaws.

Say something, she told herself, but she couldn't think of anything to say.

Kathleen said, "Mario is leaving early tomorrow, I think we'd better make a move. Hope you don't mind?"

"Of course not, who are we to stand in the way of true love?" O'Shea said. Fionn echoed his grandson.

Nessa jumped up, relieved. "Can I cadge a lift, Kathleen?"

"You don't have to get up early, do you, Nessa?" O'Shea said in his don't-spoil-things voice.

"Well no, but I...I've sold my car, and...."

"I'll leave you home, unless you have some objection...." he said.

Kathleen winked at her. Nessa conceded.

As Mario was saying goodbye to Fionn, Kathleen whispered to Nessa, "You've got him by the short and curlies, make the most of it, all this could be yours, kiddo."

Nessa laughed in spite of herself. A little laugh frilled with sadness. Nevertheless, it was a laugh. O'Shea looked at her. She lowered her eyes. Thank you God.

As O'Shea escorted Kathleen and Mario out, Fionn said, "I've something to show you."

The muscles in Nessa's heart contracted. It had

to be the box.

Pandora's box. He opened it, the same dark blue velvet lining as her own. He pulled the ribbon to open the shelf; it was empty. He opened a secret drawer housing a frail piece of parchment and a feather pen.

"I bought two of these. One for Deirdre and one for me. To keep our letters when we were apart. As you can see it's empty except for this little note she wrote the night before I left." He took it up almost reverently. "Would you like to read it?"

"No, no, I'd feel I was intruding. It was for your eyes only." She prayed he'd put it it back before O'Shea returned.

He folded the letter carefully and slowly returned it to the secret drawer.

"Yes, you're right. Deirdre's and mine," he said, pulling down the shelf.

Hurry up. Please hurry up, willed Nessa. He closed the box in slow motion.

Kept it on his knees. Fondling it.

"You bring me photographs of Deirdre, at different stages, I'll keep them in this.... Her children...even her husband."

"Yes, I will, I've loads. I'll put the box back on the table if you like."

"Thank you, my dear," he said, handing it to her. She was putting it on the table when O'Shea came in. He looked at her and at the box. Accusing her.

"I think it's time for bed, Fionn," he said gently.

"Unfortunately, yes," Fionn laughed, "I had a fine old time. Very stimulating."

O'Shea helped him up. Nessa kissed him and he

said as he went out, "Did you write to your uncle?"

"Not yet, he's in Perth. When he returns to Sydney, I'll write and ask." Should she tell him she was thinking of emigrating now that it was definitely on the cards again? He would be upset. O'Shea was right not wanting them to meet. She looked at him for guidance. His jaw was tight.

"Nessa is thinking of going to Australia."

"Emigrating?"

She nodded.

"Oh my dear, just when I found you," he said soulfully.

"I'm sorry, but I'm a bit lonely.... Oisín's my only family...I miss him and now Kay will more than likely be going...and I haven't even got the Saturday job anymore...." her voice petered out.

"Don't distress yourself my dear...only thinking of myself...old people can be very selfish...of course you must go. Family is very important, don't know what I'd do without Magda and Owen. Write to me. Fill my writing box with photographs and letters."

"Of course I will," she hugged him.

"Fionn showed me his writing box," she said to O'Shea.

"Really, how did Nessa get you to do that, Grandfather? You don't usually let anyone touch it."

"Nessa's special. I don't suppose Deirdre...." Fionn said.

Oh God he's going to ask about Gran's box...what'll I say? Yes I have the box...or lie?

O'Shea cut in, "Come on, Grandfather...."

"I will see you again, Nessa?"

"Of course, by the time I've everything sorted it'll be weeks...."

"Come and see me soon."

"I will," she said, wondering how she would if he was in Wicklow and she carless.

As O'Shea guided the old man out, Nessa asked him if she could use the phone.

"Over there," he pointed.

She rang for a taxi and gathered her things. She'd walk to the gate. No, she'd have good manners, wait and thank him. At least no fear of tears. He couldn't hurt her any more, no matter what he did or said. Her body was numb.

"Like a brandy?" he said, coming in softly.

"No thanks. I'll be going...."

"What's the rush?"

"I've overstayed my welcome."

"If you could curb your nosiness and...."

"I didn't ask about the writing box, Fionn showed...."

"So you said."

"Look, I'm not getting into an argument with you, I know what I said and did, you can interrogate your grandfather tomorrow. Pin him against the wall and extract the truth from him."

"You're being offensive."

"Just speaking from experience."

A shadow crossed his face, followed by anger. "You change with the wind."

"Me? I change like the wind? That's a laugh ...actually I don't change at all.... I'm fickle just like my gran, I'm mean and evil too, a chip off the old block...et cetera, et cetera...." She yawned.

"You don't know what it's like living with this

old man obsessed and possessed by Deirdre. She has poisoned our lives. My mother's very upset. My grandmother was a warm, wonderful human being, full of good humour. Kindness personified."

"But blighted and slighted by Fionn's love for Deirdre," Nessa said sarcastically.

"No, of course not. "

"Oh, so Deirdre's not responsible for your mother's and your traumatic childhoods?"

"We both had very happy childhoods."

"The poison didn't start working till recently then?"

"Fionn only mentioned Deirdre in the last two years. We didn't know about her till then and haven't stopped hearing about her since."

"Perfectly logical, he feels his time is running out and he can tell his story without hurting anyone. If he really was upsetting your mother, why didn't she say so? From what Fionn has told me about Magda she's not exactly a shrinking violet. It's you who's harbouring this festering hate for Deirdre. You don't happen to have an effigy of her, do you? She had terrible arthritis last year."

His nostrils flared. He looked a bit like a horse. He rolled his fists into balls. You're asking for trouble, she told herself, but couldn't stop.

"And I'm going to help him find out about Deirdre."

"Mind your own business, it's none of your concern."

"Except dastardly Deirdre is my grandmother and I'd like to know myself.... And another thing, he waited ten years after Deirdre before marrying your grandmother."

"What's that to do with anything?"

"Well, it was hardly on the rebound, unless of course you're a family of...." she was going to say retards but thought better, "extra slow movers."

O'Shea looked at her coldly.

"And your grandmother knew all about Deirdre before he married her?"

"Yes, so what?"

"And she told him about her first love killed in an accident just before she met Fionn, so they were both second best."

That shook him. He was literally speechless. She felt a bit afraid. She shouldn't have fabricated. But having told the lie, she cemented it with the truth.

"They had a lovely life according to Fionn. No grand passion, but a loving home. It doesn't sound to me like she felt hard done by. It's you, O'Shea, who's carrying the grudge At least Fionn's magnificent obsession is love. Yours is hate. Hatred of a little old dead woman."

"I'm only upset for my mother," he said feebly, "and the pain inflicted on Fionn by that *sweet* little old lady."

"And because you can't get at her, you're taking it out on me."

He didn't answer. Suddenly she felt exhausted, like a pummelled fighter who couldn't come out of his corner when the bell went for the tenth round. A cold silence crept up between them. She wanted to get up, walk to the gate, but she couldn't. All her energy was sapped. Even her tear-ducts dried up. Her feelings cut off at the nerve ends.

"Come on, I'll take you home," he said wearily.

She got up slowly, "No need."

"Shank's mare?" he jeered.

"No, wouldn't risk it—some creep might follow me."

The doorbell rang. Both jumped. O'Shea frowned. Puzzled.

"My taxi." She held out her hand. "Thank you for a delightful meal and good company."

"Pity you had to ruin everything with your snooping."

She withdrew her hand. Pain surged through her body. She wanted to tear her heart out to stop it.

As he opened the hall door, she said softly, "You've won, my spirit is in bits on the conservatory floor. Dance on it."

In the taxi, she felt she was coming apart at the seams, like her rag doll Matilda that the dog ravaged, knocking the stuffing out of it. Even when she was carefully sewn back, Matilda was never the same again. Like Nessa.

It was ironic really. She used to worry about Kathleen being hurt by some unfeeling bastard who'd abuse her childlike love and trusting nature. But Kathleen had met her Mr Wonderful who was as besotted as Kathleen herself and it was she, Nessa, who was spurned.

A sigh, long and mournful, came out involuntarily. The driver eyed her in the mirror. Oh God, don't let him be nice.

"You all right love?" he asked.

"Flu," she said.

"I'll put the heater on, have to mind the aul bronicals, wha'? The night air can be treacherous."

"Thanks," said Nessa on a gush of tears that

swept from nowhere, drowning the taxi in a sob.

"Jasus Miss, it's an ark ye need."

"Sorry."

"Some flu to cause such grief."

The tears rained down her face in a fine mist, drowning her dress.

"It...it was more like pneumonia...on the verge actually...."

"Ah, that explains it. Pneumonia often takes people like that, depresses the system, leaves ye fragile, ye know what I mean?"

Nessa said she did. She felt like an egg with a very thin shell.

"Affects the heart.... People feel very lonely in the small hours of the morning after pneumonia. Things get on top of them. Emotional, a bit like love, ye know what I mean?"

He was so kind she cried all the way home. And when they got there he made a great fuss of her, opening the car door for her, helping her out, advising her to mind herself. Even waited till she was safely in before moving off.

She took her shoes off and crept through the house followed by soft whispers wafting through the air. Exhausted, she fell into a deep dreamless sleep, awoken by a tap on the door in the morning.

"Mario is off," Kathleen said.

She jumped up, wrapped a dressing gown around her and went down to say goodbye. She hugged him, telling him how pleased she was to meet him and how happy she was for them both.

Mario said, "I had planned to introduce you to my cousin Antonio who is in need of a wife and you'd be perfect, but I see Owen O'Shea and you are like Kathleen and me."

She smiled broadly hoping the ache in her heart wasn't showing through. Nessa wished Kathleen wasn't going on to work after seeing Mario off. She wanted desperately to tell her what happened. Hoping it would ease the pain.

When they left, Nessa went back to bed and slept fitfully. Eventually she got up, made coffee and plans. Back to Plan A. Australia. Carry it through this time. No nonsense. It was ridiculous for her to hope...anyway, from now on she'd be rational, logical and, and...she ran out of words. O'Shea kept coming into her mind. O'Shea...O'Shea...she'd say it till it didn't hurt. She said it over and over, till it became just a little barb in her heart.

Now she'd make a list: Number one, write to Oisín. Tell him she was coming. Two, book her flight. She'd wait till she got to Sydney to tell him about Fionn...no, maybe...she dithered.... Should she tell him first? She'd ask Kathleen her opinion.

She went out in the back garden with a book. She didn't feel well. She couldn't concentrate. The events of the night before swirled around in her head giving her a headache. She was about to go back inside when a face appeared over the wall.

"Hoped you'd be here. I've been ringing your bell," said Danny grinning. He threw himself over, landing at Nessa's feet. She had to laugh. No longer angry with him.

"Howya?" she said.

"Great. Great."

"Barbara?"

"Gone."

"Mind...?"

"Relieved actually. I feel light with relief. Thank God she wasn't pregnant."

"Coffee?"

"Lovely."

He followed her in to the flat. They sat and chatted like the old friends they were and Nessa wanted them to stay. The doorbell rang. She stiffened.

"Will I?" said Danny.

She nodded.

He came back grinning with a bunch of pure yellow roses. "For you, Mademoiselle."

Nessa recoiled, refusing to take them.

"Don't you want them?"

"No, take them away."

"There's even a bigger bunch for Kay, red ones. Left them downstairs."

The card fell. Danny picked it up, "Who's this Mario you don't want flowers from?"

"Mario, they're from Mario?" she said, feeling foolish and a teeny weeny bit disappointed.

She took them tenderly, saying she had thought they were from someone else. Carefully arranging them in a vase she told Danny about Kathleen's Latin lover, giving Danny an opportunity to mention Europe again. That's why he'd come, to tell her his plans. He had decided to buy a rail ticket and do Europe in his two free months before the school reopened. And, as himself and Barbara were no longer an item, he might suss out job opportunities for the following year. Nessa said she thought that was a great idea. She told him she was about to book her ticket to Australia. He said he rather fancied Australia himself. She didn't look at him or answer. She didn't want to give him a sliver of hope. Too unkind.

Kathleen cried with joy and sorrow when she saw the dozen dark red velvet petalled roses. A simple note attached, *With my heart, Mario.*

For the second time in her life Nessa felt jealous of Kathleen…. The first time was when Gran brought Kathleen home. A big awkward lump, three years older than ten year old Nessa, but bchaving like a seven year old. She was timid, afraid of her shadow, always trying to please. Especially nervous of Nessa's grandfather. When he spoke to her she jumped. Not used to men. The only men she had encountered were priests. Nessa didn't mind Gran visiting Kathleen in the orphanage but when she began coming for weekends, Nessa didn't like it. Nessa didn't like her. Didn't like the attention she was getting.

Gran said she wanted them to be friends. Kathleen was willing but Nessa said she had her own friends and wouldn't let Kathleen play with her toys. Her grandfather said nothing but bought Kathleen a beautiful rag doll with a big smiling face and petticoats and pantaloons. Kathleen's face radiated pure joy as she clasped the doll to her. Nessa burned with resentment and jealousy.

"Do I get a little kiss?" her grandfather said sticking out his jaw.

Kathleen shyly pecked it and retreated. Gran and Granpa were chuffed. Later Nessa snatched the doll from Kathleen and pinched her into the bargain. Her grandmother was livid and smacked her legs and told her she was a spoilt little brat…the

only time Gran ever hit her. Kathleen said she
didn't mind if she pinched her or took her doll if
she'd play with her and be her friend, but Nessa
refused, hating her even more. Wouldn't even say
goodbye on Sunday evening.

The following Friday when Gran was going to
collect Kathleen for the weekend, Nessa refused to
accompany her and kicked up such a fuss that Gran
went on the bus while Grandpa stayed at home to
mind her. The time was long. She could feel her
grandfather's disapproval, though he said nothing.
He kept looking at his watch. Eventually he got up
saying, "Come on, Nessa, the bus will be in soon,
let's go and meet Deirdre and Kathleen." Nessa,
still cocooned in her sulk, hung back. Grandpa
gave her a look and held out his hand. Reluctantly
she took it. On the way down the road, Nessa
prayed to God to get rid of Kathleen. Kill her.

When the bus finally arrived, Gran had to be
helped off. She was white. And alone.

Nessa was delighted and terrified. Did God do
it? Did he kill Kathleen?

When Granpa put his arm around Gran she
burst into tears. Grandpa almost carried her home.

"They wouldn't let her out," Gran kept saying
over and over. "Said she was sick. They wouldn't let
me in to see her."

Nessa was glad and relieved. She prayed fervently
Kathleen would get better. Gran whispered
something to Grandpa.

"We'll see about that," he said.

He made phone calls. He shouted and threatened
and told people he'd have them in court and all
sorts of things. He said he was coming there and

then, and he a medical doctor, and he'd been on to the minister and there had better not be any excuses when he arrived.

It was the only time Nessa saw him angry. He drove straight to the orphanage and took Kathleen home with him and she never went back. She was black and blue. A nun had beaten her with a cane because she told the other children she had a family and Nessa was her sister.

Nessa blamed God for doing what she asked. Everytime she looked at battered Kathleen she cried. When Kathleen was safely, officially fostered by Gran and Grandpa, Gran went baldheaded for Sr Declan, declaring her unfit to be with children, and insisted on having her moved from the orphanage. Eventually she got her way.

Gran continued to visit the orphanage. Grandpa always accompanied her. When Kathleen was about two months living with them, Gran asked her would she like to visit her favourite nun, Sr Brigid, but Kathleen shrank into a corner and screamed and screamed. Then Gran asked Sr Brigid to visit them one Sunday. She came bringing two little girls with her. Kathleen hid. They continued to come once a month. Eventually, when her confidence grew and she knew she wasn't going back, Kathleen looked forward to the visits and mothered the little girls. She kept up the friendship with Sr Brigid till the nun died.

Nessa became Kathleen's champion, but the guilt of that time remained with Nessa long after she accepted and loved Kathleen as a sister....

"Kay, I'm so glad and envious," she said hugging

her extra hard.

"Oh Nessa, I can't believe this is happening to me.... There's something else...two tickets to Sardinia...one each...for you and me...just a week. Everything provided...free accommodation in luxurious apartments attached to Mario's cousin's hotel...."

"Don't ask, Kay, I couldn't. "

"O'Shea," Kathleen sighed, "You don't want to leave Owen...don't blame you."

"I want to get as far away from him as I can...he's, he's.... Oh Kay...." She began to cry great mournful sobs like in the taxi. Kathleen held her in her arms. Nessa told her about O'Shea. Everything, except what he'd said about Deirdre. Kathleen, incredulous, blue eyes opened as wide as her mouth. Then her mouth snapped shut, her eyes bulged.

"You've got to come, Nessa. I couldn't leave you pining for that total shithead...."

Nessa laughed. "I'd love to but I'd be the biggest gooseberry in Sardinia."

"There's always Antonio, Mario's cousin...."

"Matchmaking again, you can't stop can you? *Read my lips*...*No, No, No*. I mightn't even *like* Antonio and he might hate me and we'll be thrown together...I couldn't...."

"Oh yes you could...look what happened to me."

"OK, on two conditions: I don't have to go anywhere with you and Mario...."

"I promise, not even if you change your mind and beg."

"...And Antonio, you don't try to fix me up with Antonio."

"Would I do such a thing?"

"Yes. Promise."

"I promise not to interfere with nature. It won't be my fault if the pair of you fall head over heels."

"Kathleen, shut it."

"OK...you'll come?"

"I've a check up today—if all's well, I'll go."

"Oh Nessa, we'll have a wonderful time; sand, sea and sex. You won't think twice about O'Shea."

"I'll settle for the sand and sea."

"OK, OK."

Kathleen raced off, leaving Nessa brooding. Sardinia, I'm off to Sardinia, sun and sea. O'Shea snuck into her mind. She felt herself hardening. He had such a negative effect on her. She tried to convince herself she was lucky she had encountered his dark side.

CHAPTER SIX

"So you want to go to Sardinia...?" Doctor O'Brien said, putting away his stethoscope.

"I do, for a week."

"Your lungs are fine. Keep out of the sun. No sunbathing whatsoever."

"OK," she said lightly.

He looked over his glasses, "I mean it...."

She nodded.

"Stay under cover, and when you swim use total block and wrap up immediately."

"Yes, Doc."

"Sardinia.... Why Sardinia?"

She told him about Kathleen and Mario and the roses and tickets and everything.

He sighed, "Young love, can't beat it.... Seen O'Shea lately?"

"Had dinner at his place the other night."

"Had you indeed?" he said, dying for facts. He waited. She didn't elaborate. She was giving him mind-your-own-business looks but he wasn't noticing.

"How did it go?" His face full of enthusiasm.

She relented. "It was wonderful for a time.... Mario, Kathleen, Fionn and O'Shea.... Everyone in great form, good wine and food, stimulating

conversation. And fun, plenty of fun. Fionn was
thrilled, kept patting my hand and O'Shea was
massive. I couldn't take my eyes off him.... I felt like
a little glow-worm, my feelings shining through
every pore. He couldn't but see it. At one stage I felt
he was even responding...." She stalled.

"Yes, yes," said Doctor O'Brien impatiently.

"Well, towards the end of the night I could see
his mood changing, looking to pick a fight...actually
I think there's something wrong with O'Shea,
definitely has a split personality."

"O'Shea's as solid as a rock," Doctor O'Brien
said, chuckling.

"He accused me of spoiling the night by my
nosiness and I was only looking at Fionn's writing
box because Fionn insisted on showing it to me...."

The doctor bent forward conspiritorally. "You
know what this means...?" he said

"Yeah...either schizophrenia or just a plain nasty
bit of work."

He gave a big guffaw slapping his knee. "I knew
this would happen...could see it coming...knew
you'd do it.... O'Shea's afraid of you."

"Ah come off it, Doc."

"He's afraid he's falling in love with you and
he's fighting it...he can't bear the thought of ending
up like his grandfather...obsessed.... He's seen the
power...what you could do to him...."

"Who are you kidding?"

"It's hard for a man like O'Shea, always in
control, calling the shots, then a slip of a thing like
you...."

"Stop right there...before I end up feeling sorry
for the brute...."

"Better than bitter."

"You don't realise what this this bastard has done to me, he's crushed my spirit. He's left my heart in tatters," she said, starting to cry.

"Sorry, I didn't realise.... I'm an insensitive oaf.... Sardinia will do you a power of good, best medicine you could have at the moment. Heal the damage in no time."

"My lungs...."

"Your lungs will be fine if you follow my instructions. I'm not talking about your lungs, I'm talking about healing your heart. Maybe O'Shea isn't right for you but don't let him sour other relationships that are yet to come. Otherwise you'll end up a cold fish."

"I think it's too late, Doc," Nessa sniffed. "My heart is already shrivelling up. I can feel it contracting."

"Nonsense, I'm surprised at you, Nessa, letting that man upset you like that," he said, adding stupidly, "There's plenty more fish in the sea."

"Well that's good news, seeing I'm going to end up a cold fish."

He laughed with her. "That's the girl, still have your sense of humour."

"You know what they say about the clown."

"So many people suffering from heartache and the only medicine a physician can offer is advice...." he sighed a great guttural sigh. "Inadequate advice to heal the misery of heartache."

"I needed to tell someone, even if I didn't want to. Thanks for listening"

"The next time I see O'Shea, I'll give him a piece of my mind," he pledged.

She fluttered. "Oh no...please...don't, don't mention me...promise?"

"Very well...my lips are sealed...but what that bucko needs is a good kick up the arse...."

Coming out of the St. Stephen's Green centre with her prescribed long-sleeved cotton shirts and long skirts, Nessa saw a vision moving along towards Grafton Street with Fionn in tow. If it wasn't Joseph in his amazing multicoloured dream coat, in drag, it had to be Magda. Bottle black hair cascaded down the back of an incredible ankle-length coat of many colours. Bangles clanged and tinkled as she moved through the crowd. Nessa's mouth was still hanging in a gawk when Fionn saw her.

"Nessa," he said, his leathery old face crinkling.

Nessa moved shyly forward consumed in a red blush.

Magda grabbed her, holding her at bejewelled and bespangled arms' length.

"Nessa, granddaughter of Deirdre," she said in a threatrical gush, pulling her forward, scrutinizing her to the amusement of onlookers and mortification of Nessa. "The genes of the grandmother passed on almost intact...."

Nessa waited.

"Except for the nose of course...."

The nose, of course, the bloody nose...Nessa Cyrano Walsh, that's me. Nessa sizzled.

"I *must* paint your face, like my father painted your grandmother," Magda was bellowing.

Nessa wanted to hit her.

"We must talk. I can't paint anyone unless I know them intimately.... Get the *feeeel*,"she said, squeezing Nessa.

Off the wall, completely and utterly, Nessa concluded, eyeing the mascara cascading over the puffy eye bags and glutting in Magda's wrinkles. She looked at Fionn who rolled his eyes.

"'Fraid you're out of luck, I'm off to Sardinia day after tomorrow and when I return, it's Australia," Nessa said with relish.

"Australia, Australia, but why?" Magda roared.

"Because I want to." She tried to stop the ice forming on her voice for Fionn's sake, as her face set like a barometer at frost.

"Then there's no time to lose. Come, follow me."

And Nessa did, like a tug bobbing along behind a majestic ocean liner, as Magda moved down Grafton Street, parting the crowd and sailing towards The Westbury. She stood in the doorway making her presence felt with a superb stare, then advanced, sweeping haughtily through the foyer, leaving Fionn smiling to left and right healing any offence Magda may have caused.

"We shall have lunch," Magda declared to everybody and nobody in particular. Nessa said she wasn't hungry.

"Nonsense," said Magda, "after all you've been through. You need proper food."

A waiter escorted them to their table and gave them a menu each. Nessa looked at Fionn who winked at her conspiratorially.

A monster, Nessa decided. Magda was a monster with a capital M. No wonder O'Shea was fucked up.

Magda recommended the vegetarian lasagne she was having herself and Nessa conceded. Fionn had a steak. Nessa grudgingly admitted it was good and wolfed it down. Over coffee Magda again examined Nessa's face.

"You have an even better face than Deirdre, more character. Stronger. Better for the bit of imperfection...."

"My nose?" said Nessa.

"Of course."

"As soon as I get a few bob together I'm having a nose job."

"How could you?" screeched Magda. "It's so vulgar, everyone and anyone has one of those cute little retrousse noses, they're even doing them on the National Health.... Do you want to look like everyone else?"

"No, it's...I'm conscious of the bump and, and...." Nessa muttered.

"Rubbish, you are all the better for it. It's a fine nose, isn't it, Fionn?"

"Yes, indeed it is, but I have to take issue with you, Nessa hasn't got a better face than Deirdre— they are both lovely."

"And I'd like a nose like hers."

"That settles it, I *must* paint you before you're *ruined*," Magda thundered.

Fionn butted in, "Nessa has a right...."

"Even if she's about to destroy herself...look at her, does she need improving?"

"No, she's fine but she has a right...."

"Beauty is in the eye of the beholder. And we who eye her have a right to tell her she doesn't need mutilation."

Jeeesus Christ let me out of here, thought Nessa.

"Maybe I'll reconsider," she said to stop Magda

exploding.

"Wonderful, that's absolutely wonderful." She hugged Nessa warmly, almost motherly. "Have some rose-hip tea."

As she poured, Magda said, "You know, Nessa, we have had the divine Deirdre for breakfast, dinner and tea for the past two years. Tragic as it is, I had to call a halt. I threatened to ban her name unless Fionn did something.... Go out and find her, I said. He tried but, alas, it was too late."

She squeezed Fionn's hand affectionately. "I was delighted when he told me about you, at least you were another dimension, now tell me all about yourself."

Nessa's face flamed scarlet.

"Better do it fast, or Magda will tell you all about herself and you'll be sorry," warned Fionn.

"Why would she be sorry, I had a very interesting life, I should write a book about my experiences. If I did it certainly would be a bestseller. But I haven't the time. Anyway, I need to concentrate on my art."

"If you put as much energy into painting the canvas as painting the town, you'd be far more prolific," Fionn said.

"I can only paint when seized by the muse and I'm seized now. I *must* paint Nessa.... Kismet...do you believe in kismet...?

"Well, I...."

"We were destined to meet, I will immortalize you on canvas.... People beg me to paint them, mostly I refuse...I have to get that feeling, the adrenalin flowing...I have it now...I can't waste it.... You *must* come to Wicklow for a day even...I *need* you.... I'll send Rory to collect you at half eight in the morning."

"No, sorry, I can't."

"But you're exactly what I need, I *must* have you."

"Susan! Why not paint Owen's girlfriend?"

"*Susan*, definitely not, too pretty. I need spirit, fire...passion."

"Sorry, afraid you'll have to find another Cyrano."

Grabbing Nessa.... "I'm sorry if I've offended you...I love your nose, it's different."

If she doesn't stop I'm going to sock her one, Nessa thought, struggling free.

"Fionn, *do* something," Magda commanded

"Right," said Fionn, calling the waiter. He came.

"Ask the chef to slice off this young lady's head and serve it to Salome here on a plate."

"Garnished or ungarnished?" said the waiter po-faced.

"Any suggestions?"

"A sprig of rosemary, perhaps?"

"Excellent."

Nessa began to laugh and couldn't stop. Fionn joined her. Magda, on the verge of a sulk, changed her mind and hooting, ordered champagne.

"A day, one little day," Magda coaxed as Nessa weakened with every sip of champagne.

Nessa had to admit there was nothing earth-shattering to be done and heard herself agreeing to go to Wicklow. Magda was magnanimous, thanking her profusely. Afraid Magda might blow it, Fionn side-tracked her.

"Magda's husband is making quite a name for

himself, too," he said.

Nessa noted the too.

"Yes, my husband is a wonderful man, saving the earth."

"Solo," Fionn jeered.

"Have you seen him on telly, in the Amazon rain-forest?"

"No I'm afraid I haven't."

"Where have you been? Anyone who's anyone is talking about it."

"Magda opens her dinner-party conversation with 'My husband the anthropologist, as seen on television.'"

Nessa sniggered.

"You may well laugh but I'm very proud of him—not many women have such husbands."

"He's a good man, all right."

"I don't have a television," Nessa said.

"A cultural decision on your part?"

"You could say that," Nessa lied. She wasn't going to confess it was repossessed when she fell behind on the payments.

"I too, do my bit for the world. My vegetarianism didn't come easy...for a full-blooded carnivore like me it was a sacrifice. A great sacrifice. I still hanker over juicy rare steaks with the blood running."

Bubbling with champagne, tiny giggles burst from Nessa as she pictured Magda gnawing through a raw leg of beef.

Half-formed words burst and tippled into titters from her. She watched them watching her but couldn't stop. They put her in a taxi and waved her off. She giggled all the way home.

Rory called the next morning in a jeep, as grey cloud matted the sky sending down a slow drizzle.

"Magda will not be pleased," Rory said, sucking air through his teeth.

"Tough," said Nessa.

"If Magda's not pleased, everyone suffers, especially her sitter."

"Oh yeah? Well here's one who won't take it."

"You'll take it. Everyone does."

"Right then, I'm not coming. Tell her I changed my mind."

Fright lightened the freckles on his face. "Don't do this to me, Nessa, she'll blame me and I owe her...."

"Well I don't, and I don't have to put up with her tantrums."

"Please come with me so that I've done my bit, and if she throws a wobbly you can say or do what you like and I'll bring you straight back if you want."

"Promise?"

"Promise."

"Right, but any shit from Magda and I'm off."

The rain settled to a permanent drizzle, dragging the sky almost to their heads. Nessa tried to converse but Rory couldn't get beyond the weather. She gave up. They drove in grey blanket silence except for Rory's odd curse at the skies. Into Wicklow the sky began to lighten. So did Rory, and when the sun burst through he was full of aul chat.

"So it's just the two of us," Nessa said.

"What?"

"Sitting for Magda."

"I'm not sitting. She's done me lots of times,

well different bits of me."

"Then why are you coming?"

"I got the call. When Magda calls I drop everything and come."

"What do you do?"

"This, that and the other," he laughed. "A jack of all trades."

Jeeesus Christ, he must be her toy-boy. She sneaked a look at him. He was young, fit, a real clean-cut, healthy type.

"Magda's a pain at times but she's been very good to me, through her I got all my clients."

Nessa kept these things locked in her head. She mightn't even tell Kathleen.

Magda was charming, hugging both of them and thanking her for coming and Rory for delivering Nessa so promptly. He excused himself saying he had to look after his babies.

The house was unlike anything she had seen before; outside, a fairy story with thatched roof and an old fashioned garden overgrown with hollyhocks, foxgloves and decadent roses rambling all over the place. All kinds of everything, including an aromatic herb garden. The studio was apart from the cottage in a wood. A house of glass. Honeysuckle, wisteria, ivy creepers, clematis, clambered up its sides. Rain-drops kept falling on their heads from glistening leaves as they crunched their way through the trees to the studio. The ground floor was totally bare. Probably a gallery, a show piece for her work. Upstairs, via a winding staircase, was the studio. The view over the lakes and to the mountains was breathtaking.

"Wear these," Magda said, handing Nessa

Hollywood-style gypsy clothes that no self respecting gypsy would be seen dead in.

"I thought it was a head and shoulders."

"Yes, but I must get the all over picture, the feel."

Nessa felt the resentment rippling along her frills and flounces and her face setting in a scowl.

"Stay easy, just like that and look at me...."

Nessa looked at her hard.

"I am a gypsy in my soul, full of wanderlust...." said Magda, mixing her paints.

"Maybe you were in a previous existence."

"There is no maybe about it.... I am out of my time...always knew I was a nomad...certain I was adopted.... Such ordinary people couldn't have begotten me."

"Maybe there was a mix-up in the hospital and...."

"No, I investigated that possibility. I'm the spit of my mother, in looks anyway...unfortunately I was born at home.... You can imagine my disappointment when I discovered I was their real flesh and blood...of course lots of geniuses come from quite ordinary parents."

"Yes," said Nessa, feeling her lip curling in a sneer as Magda took up her brush.

"Don't move until I tell you," Magda ordered.

Nessa's resentment burned into the canvas. Magda didn't seem to notice. She worked wildly as if in a trance.

Stiff and hungry, after what seemed like ten hours, Nessa pleaded for a break.

"Soon," Magda said.

An hour later, she stopped. Nessa was exhausted.

They trudged back to the cottage. Rory appeared, saying, "Ladies, your herbal bath awaits." Magda showed Nessa to the bathroom. A big Victorian bath, steaming and strewn with herbs and petals, stood in the middle of a huge bathroom. One huge bath.... Sharing with Magda...I am not sharing a bath with Magda under any circumstances, Nessa decided.

"You have it, Magda, you did all the work, I was only standing."

"They also serve who only stand and wait...we both need it. It's not as if there's only one, if that was the case of course I'd get it. Mine's next door in my ensuite. Hurry up and enjoy...lunch will be in a half hour."

"Thank you," said Nessa, chastened.

"Do you want your massage before or after lunch?"

"Massage?"

"Nothing compares to Rory's massage. He has such a light touch."

"You make him sound like a pastry cook."

"He's that too, as good with kneading dough as flesh. He was a chef before he became a masseur. He looks after my herb garden and he's prepared lunch."

"A man for all seasons."

"And reasons," laughed Magda. "Before or after?"

"Neither, the bath will suffice...."

"You don't know what you're missing...."

Oh yeah, thought Nessa, with the sure knowledge of what she was missing. Lowering herself into the delicious smelling bath, she felt like Cleopatra. Soft music drifted over her from next door. Lolling in the pure hedonistic luxury she could hear little squeals of joy wafting along the music. Magda was enjoying her massage.... Am I a prude, Nessa asked herself, and was shocked to realise she probably was. She dozed...heard a voice...low...deep. She opened her eyes and her ears.

"Hello, anyone there?" said the voice from beyond the door...his voice...O'Shea.... Her heart crackled and went into overdrive, thumping wildly off her breastbone. She could hear him breathing at the other side of the door, making her feel vulnerable, naked.

She climbed out of the bath with hardly a slurp, wrapped herself in a fat towel and waited, goosepimpling.

"It's me, Owen...?"

She held her breath as his voice opened the wound like a dry pea-pod splitting. She expected to see her heart bleeding through the towel. She wanted tears to wash away the hurt. But not a drop was forthcoming. Would she always be like that? She dragged up his nastiness. Every vicious thing he ever said. But she was not comforted and she didn't cry.

"Owen?" Rory's surprised voice from down the corridor....

"Rory, how are things?" O'Shea said, friendly, his footsteps walking away towards Rory. Nessa heard them talking, but not what they were saying. They laughed. Footsteps moving further away.

Her clothes stuck to wet patches as she dressed too quickly. She sat wondering and starving, her flounces wilting in the damp. She'd never have come if she'd known he was still in the country. A knock on the door. She stiffened.

"Nessa, lunch is ready," Rory said.

Nessa came out cautiously, bracing herself to face O'Shea. No sign of him. In the kitchen Magda and Fionn were seated at a table adorned with bowls of yellow and blue flowers. Fionn was in great form, delighted to see Nessa as she was to see him. No sign of O'Shea. Rory served fennel soup and Nessa ate it greedily. No mention of O'Shea. Did she imagine it?

After the main course of red dragon pie, Magda said Nessa really must have a massage. Nessa's bald "NO" took them all by surprise. She softened it saying the bath had totally refreshed her.

"I always find the massage even more benefical," Magda said.

From the sounds emanating from the adjoining room, Nessa could well believe it.

After lunch, they went back to the studio while Fionn said he'd potter in the garden with Rory and then have a nap. Ready for the fun and games. A crowd were coming in the evening. Rory's partner was going to help him massage. Nessa thought she would like to be a fly on the wall but had no intention of participating.

"Did you see Owen?" Magda asked, attempting to put life back into Nessa's drooping flounces.

"No."

"Rory told me he dropped in, but when he told Owen I was working with a sitter he left. He's such a wonderful son, I don't deserve him."

Oh you do, you do, Nessa thought, you more than deserve each other. Magda prattled on about

Rory's delicate touch as she mixed her paints.

"He is so beautiful...such delicate hands, such a wonderful masseur.... Adoring clients beg for it.... You really would have profitted after standing for hours."

"Mmm."

"Of course he treats me extra-special. It was my suggestion he'd do the course. Qualified with flying colours. Don't tell him I said this, but Pat, his partner, is even better."

I'm going to puke if this narcissistic aul bag doesn't shut up, and what's more, if I do I'll aim for the canvas, thought Nessa.

Magda droned on, then suddenly stopped and began painting furiously as Nessa's lips zipped.

Wouldn't be surprised if Magda had an orgy planned for the evening. Well, she was getting out of there as fast as she could.

As soon as the session was over, Nessa insisted she had to leave to get ready for the morning. Reluctantly, they let her go.

"You're going to miss the best bit," Magda scolded.

"I think I can live without it," Nessa smiled.

Another minute of Magda and she wouldn't be responsible for her actions.

"Did she put your back up?" Rory asked as they drove towards Dublin.

"What?"

"Were you grinding your teeth and wanting to punch her?"

Was he looking in the window watching her from the bushes?

"Well a bit...especially after lunch."

"Bet you resented the gear," he chuckled.

"Yes, I did, as a matter of fact."

"Magda deliberately upsets her sitters so she can get the desired effect."

"What?"

"Haven't you seen her paintings?"

"No."

"She's not into pretty portraits, all are venom personified."

"She actually wanted to antagonize me?"

"Yep."

"She's sick."

"If she told you to look cross, would you?"

"Well...."

"Better to make you angry. Capture the raw hatred...."

"Not exactly hatred, more loathing."

"Is there a difference?"

"Not really, I suppose."

"Bet she kept on about the massage, saw that it bugged you."

Fuck, thought Nessa, I've played right into her hands.

"Pity, you really would have enjoyed the massage.... I'm supposed to have the right touch."

"Job satisfaction is a wonderful thing," Nessa said sarcastically.

Rory didn't notice. "Can't wait to get going on this crowd, a real challenge, getting them tuned up for the craic. Never had so many at one time, mini-marathon."

"Sorry for dragging you away."

"No problem, Pat will start if I'm not back in

time. I'm good, but Pat's even better. Has the magic touch. Poetry in motion, Magda says...."

"Praise indeed."

"Magda is something else.... Started me down a new road. I always think of my life as BM and AM; before and after Magda."

"How extraordinary."

"She has that effect on most people."

"True, she's definitely memorable, but I wouldn't go that far."

"She asked me 'specially to come to massage you so you wouldn't be tired for the afternoon session."

"Did she? Sorry I disappointed you."

"You didn't—no skin off my nose, it's not for everyone."

"Magda was very insistent."

"Only for your own good...very refreshing.... Instead she annoyed you...worked out better for her. Didn't have to look for something to goad you."

"Definitely a split personality."

She felt like ringing Magda and apologising for thinking she was an obnoxious, overbearing, egotistical asshole...when she was actually an overbearing, egotistical nutcase. She smiled.

"What are they going to do that they need massages to start?"

"Now that would be telling...." he said smiling, turning on a tape.

CHAPTER SEVEN

Mario was waiting at the airport, his eyes misting with love for Kathleen. A sliver of envy touched Nessa's heart, surprising her. Her heart was not altogether dead. Mario hugged Nessa and kissed Kathleen passionately. They drove for a few miles before entering the ancient walled town of Alghero with churches rising majestically above the maze of narrow cobbled streets. Most of the buildings were so old they had the texture of pale crumbling biscuits.

Their hotel was about a mile outside the town, past the fishing port and marina.... Suddenly the sea was curtained off by masses of trees.

God, Nessa thought, it's greener than Ireland.

The hotel was set in whispering foliage of exotic palms and peach trees and all sort of strange plants Nessa had never seen before. The hotel foyer was coolly elegant in dark blue and white marble. Glass-topped tables were wrapped by sumptuous deep navy leather couches.

Behind the reception desk was the most beautiful man Nessa had ever seen, dressed in charcoal grey suit and white shirt. All the women tourists were gaping at him, the older ones admired him from afar. The younger ones edged closer. Three pretty dolly-birds buzzed around the desk, asking his opinion on everything and anything; cards, tours, post, souvenirs, anything to engage his attention. He was kind and polite, but distant. Nessa supposed he'd have to be. If he gave them the slightest encouragement they'd be over the counter. He wasn't arrogant either. More shy...no, not shy, embarrassed...no...resigned. That was it. When the girls ran out of questions they reluctantly left, but still hovered around the foyer.

Mario went over to the desk.

"Well," said Kathleen, "what do you think of him?"

"Adonis," Nessa sighed.

"Even better looking than O'Shea?"

"Definitely...he's almost too good-looking."

"Too good-looking! Wouldn't hold it against him."

"I said *almost*...just look at those little groupies...rapt. Hope they're not disappointed when they meet the rest of Sardinia's manhood."

"Yeah, "said Kathleen. "Pity they saw him first."

"How could any one follow that?"

"Glad you think so—that's *him*, the one you didn't want to be stuck with."

"Antonio...that's Antonio...the one in need of a wife?" Nessa burst out laughing. "He's more in need of a bodyguard than a wife."

While Mario was talking to him, Antonio was looking in their direction. They came over to Nessa and Kathleen, followed by all the female eyes in the foyer.

Antonio kissed Kathleen on both cheeks. Mario introduced him to Nessa.

"Buenvenito to Alghero." He kissed her hand. Nessa's heart made a little pitter-patter sound and her stomach rumbled. She hoped he hadn't heard. She was glad she'd stopped biting her nails. The teenagers were giving her envious looks spiked with hatred.

"Nessa...." he said, lightly touching her hair, "...with the wild hair." Then smiled. A warm wonderful smile.

He called the boy to bring their cases, excused himself and went back to the desk. The young girls crowded around again.

Mario, Nessa and Kathleen followed a path, scented by honeysuckle and roses tumbling over the wall, to apartments behind the hotel. The apartment was spacious with two bedrooms like most apartments, except this one had flowers everywhere. A Mario touch. To give Kathleen and Mario space, Nessa put on her bikini under her skirt and T-shirt and said she'd go across the road to the sea. Kathleen and Nessa arranged to meet at the pool for lunch.

Behind pine-fringed sand dunes lay miles of almost deserted white sandy beach, save for a few beach boys playing football. Even they, with their tight bronzed bodies, looked like an ad in a brochure. They called to her as she paddled on the edge of the sea, so she retreated.

Lying beside the pool on a sunbed shaded by an umbrella made of straw, a faint breeze nuzzled her. It reminded her of that day in June...the day of the auction.... That day stamped in her head in black and white...every single thing that happened. Looking at the pure blue sky, she thought gratefully, at least here there was no chance of a downpour to ruin everything.

"Are you all right...?"Antonio appeared at her side, making her jump.

"Yes I'm fine, thank you."

"Making room for the passionate ones...?" he grinned.

"Yes, I feel like a bit of a gooseberry...."

"A gooseberry, never...a rose, yes."

She smiled at him...what a really nice man he was. He had everything.

"I have to go back in. If you need anything, I'll be at reception. Be careful, don't get burnt."

"I promise."

She fell asleep...dreaming of the god-like Antonio....

Her toes were tingling.... She opened her eyes.... The vision was leaning over her...the man of her dreams....

"Mmm," she murmured, reaching out, touching his face.... She woke completely on feeling his warm flesh and sat up, whipping her hand back. Turning beetroot she said, "Sorry I...I...." She couldn't say anything else. She could hardly tell him she was dreaming of him.

He laughed. "I saw you asleep in a halo of curls...with your toes sticking out.... The sun has moved. Mario told me to keep an eye on you, said you mustn't burn."

"Thanks."

"I brought this," He held up a jar, "This cream will soothe them but they probably will still blister...what a shame...."

He began gently massaging the cream on her

feet. "You will have to go barefoot.... The barefoot madonna...."

"Like in the films...?"

He looked puzzled.

"Madonna, the singer/actress mega-star ?"

"No, like in a painting.... A Raphael madonna.... The madonna with the wild hair."

Kathleen crept up on Antonio. "Oh-ho...into sucking toes, are we, Antonio?" Kathleen asked seductively.

"I'll tell you what I was doing to Nessa if you tell what you've been doing with Mario."

Kathleen blushed almost purple. Nessa giggled.

"Ciao, Nessa, Kathleen...I must go back."

"Thank you Antonio...I appreciated that," Nessa said. He smiled.

"That shook you Kay, you'll think before embarrassing Antonio again."

"Antonio is almost beyond embarrassment.... The things that women say to him even at the reception desk...talk about sexual harrassment...he's propositioned at least once every day."

"I can imagine...."

They ordered drinks. They came clinking with ice in frosted glasses. The pool's deep turquoise smooth glass shattered occasionally by divers sending myriads of jewelled lights into the air, along with wafts of Ambre Solaire mixed with chlorine.

"I've brought the towels, let's swim," Kathleen said.

"Here, or in the sea?"

"Here in the pool."

Kathleen was a good swimmer, able to dive off

the top diving-board. Nessa was more cautious. Once as a small child she almost drowned. She still remembered sitting on the river bed of the Boyne. While not exactly frightening, it was a very strange feeling, but from then on she couldn't bear water up her nose. She could never put her face down in the water. Even though she could swim quite well she still had a healthy respect for it.

They ate lunch al fresco at the bar behind them.

"Look at me Nessa...can you honestly believe someone like Mario would fall in love with me...?" Before Nessa could answer she continued, "I'm so happy, I'm afraid."

"Mario feels the same about you as you do about him. Be glad."

"Oh I am, Nessa, I am.... I'm not going to sour it by worrying will it last...he's all that I want, all that I ever wanted and to know that he loves me.... I asked him, you know...he was a perfect gentleman...didn't ask. I asked him on the last day of my holiday. I loved him...wanted him and I thought I might never see him again and I wanted a memory at least...so I asked him and he said yes...."

"You did the right thing, Kathleen...."

"Yes, I did, didn't I? I'll love that man with my dying breath...just knowing he loves me now is all I need. I could die happy at this minute...." Kathleen sighed.

"What's wrong, Kathleen?"

"The family...you know...meeting the family tonight. What if they don't like me?"

"Why shouldn't they?"

"They mightn't like foreigners...they could have

had someone lined up for Mario...might want him to marry his own...."

"Just play it by ear...he must be serious if you're meeting the family. I'll be there to back you up. Who's coming?"

"All the family...extended...brothers, sisters, grandparents, uncles, aunts—the whole shebang...."

"Where does he come in the family?"

"Second son, he's three sisters, they're all in the catering business."

"At least he's not number one son...you're not taking the heir.... Anyway it's not as if you'd be asking him to leave Sardinia or anything...."

"Yeah, yeah, true...there's something else," she looked away, then back at Nessa, pleading, "I want to tell them you're my cousin."

"That's no problem...I'd be proud to claim you as a cousin...but I don't think you should...bad start...." Nessa said, worried.

Kathleen fiddled with her hair.

"Did you tell Mario I was your cousin?"

"Not exactly...sort of hinted at it...." Tears gathered in Kathleen's eyes. "Nessa, you don't know what it's like, it's an awful affliction not knowing who you are." She brushed away a tear with the back of her hand.

"You know I'm a terrible liar, Kathleen. Haven't the face for it, as Gran used to say. A slip of the tongue could cause you and Mario a lot of pain. You'd live in fear of being found out...a casual question about your family and you'd read all sorts of things into it. Secrets make people ill."

"I know, I know, Nessa, but what if he rejects me?"

"Because you haven't a cousin? Don't be silly, Mario loves you for the fine person you are...."

"I suppose.."

"What exactly did you tell him?"

"I didn't actually tell him anything...except ...except...I was an orphan...no family. I sorta took your background for mine."

"Ah Kathleen, you'll have to tell him the truth...your birth cert....say if your mother turns up in a few years—what then?"

"Nessa! My mother doesn't want to be found. Didn't leave a crumb. Remember when I was eighteen, the big search Gran organized? Not a shred. I have no past, sometimes I used to think I was invented."

"I'm not talking about *you* looking, what if your mother decides to find you?"

"That'd be the day."

"Circumstances change, she could decide to tell her husband...or say if she became a widow...all sort of things happen...probably still fretting about you...."

"Your toes are beginning to swell," Kathleen said abruptly, closing the subject.

"So they are, they look like little pink slugs."

"Are they sore?"

"A bit. Thank God for Antonio.... I had fallen asleep, another fifteen minutes and they'd be well cooked.... The cream is very soothing...nothing to worry about...they'll stick out through my sandals...."

"Hope no one treads on them."

"I'll scream my head off if they do...look Kathleen, would...would you like me to tell Mario?"

"No."

"I'll be your cousin if that's what you want even though I don't feel like it.... I feel more like your sister."

Kathleen said nothing and they gathered their things and went back to the apartment for a siesta.

Through the wall, Nessa could hear Kathleen sobbing. Mind your own business, she told herself.... Don't interfere.... It's Kathleen's choice. The only thing to do is back her whatever she says, even if it's a lie. They'd have to synchronise stories.

She fell asleep.

When she awoke the place had a deserted feel about it.

"Kathleen," she shouted in the emptiness.... Kathleen was gone.

Nessa jumped up, alarmed. Kathleen's words about dying happy hit her in the face.... Stop, she told herself, stop adding two and two and getting ninety-six. Kathleen wouldn't do anything silly...of course not, she said, as she laced her trainers... probably gone for.... She couldn't think of anything she'd be gone for.... Then running out, she called Kathleen's name over the empty road to the pine trees.... It was all her fault.... Why couldn't she have left it...be her cousin...no big deal. Mario or his family probably would never find out and Kathleen's mother would hardly trace her to Sardinia.... Oh God Oh God....

She raced through the pine trees to the sea.... Kathleen was standing in the blue green water up to her knees in her yellow dress....

"Kathleen, Kathleen...." Nessa shouted,

ploughing through the thick soft sand...then faster on the hard wet ribs. Kathleen didn't move.

"Don't Kathleen...I'll be anything you want...lie through my teeth, I'll practise," Nessa said breathless, wading in.

Kathleen turned.

"That won't be necessary, ye aul eejit...." Kathleen said, her face radiant. "I told him and ...Nessa, he didn't care.... He didn't care."

She splashed Nessa, a huge splash right in the middle of Nessa's astonished face. Nessa, when she got her breath back, pushed Kathleen headlong into a huge wave. They splashed, pushing and shoving each other and, finally joining hands, danced around in the sea, the way they did in Bettystown when they were children.

Like two half-drowned things, they made their way back to the apartment, thankful they hadn't to drip through the hotel. They had almost made it unseen when the man from the apartment below them, sitting on his veranda, looked at them questioningly.

"Couldn't resist the emerald sea," Kathleen shouted up at him.

His mouth opened in a smile showing the biggest set of teeth either had ever seen. "Jaws," they christened him.

They showered, washed their hair and painted their finger and toenails. Kathleen was hyper. Kept putting her make up on and scrubbing it off, then changing dresses.

"What did you wear when you met Mario?" Nessa said, exasperated.

"The pale blue."

"Wear it," Nessa ordered. "I'll do your make up and God help you if you touch it, OK?"

"Yes Miss, cer'ain'y Miss."

"Have you got the present?"

"Yes Miss, here Miss, Waterford glass vase, Miss. That all right, Miss?"

"Cut the crap or I'll do you up like a tart."

"You'll make a right little schoolmarm...."

"If I could get a job.... How are we getting there?" Nessa asked, colouring Kathleen's eyelids.

"Antonio's bringing us."

Standing back from Kathleen, looking at her handiwork, Nessa said, "A terrible beauty is born."

"Bitch," said Kathleen, examining herself in the mirror. Pleased, she said, "Did a great job there."

Nessa wore a white linen dress and little gold sandals that consisted of a few straps. Perfect for small, fat, burnt toes. Kathleen and Nessa boosted each other's morale with compliments.

"We sound like a mutual admiration society," Nessa said.

"Yeah, but sure we might as well.... Nessa...you didn't really think I was going to drown myself?"

"Of course not...you'd be more into drowning your sorrows with a bottle of...."

"Gran was right, you should never lie...you're like...."

"OK, OK, point taken. But what was I to think, after listening to you bawling your head off and then going missing and finding you standing in the middle of the ocean in your dress and...."

"I was cooling off...anyway I'm grateful you were willing to lie for me, even if you're no good at it."

"Thanks very much," said Nessa, peeved. Kathleen swooped on Nessa, hugging her breathless. "Thanks, little sister."

Antonio arrived dressed in a cream silk suit, leaving Nessa gobsmacked. "How are your little toes, Nessa?" he asked, looking at them bulging out of the sandals like little cocktail sausages about to burst.

"Ready for sucking," hooted Kathleen before Nessa could reply.

Nessa dug her fist into Kathleen's back making her snuffle with titters. "You're going to ruin your mascara, Kathleen," said Nessa, bringing Kathleen under immediate control. Antonio smiled a charming smile.

Mario met them at the door and proudly escorted Kathleen in. Antonio took Nessa's arm.

The restaurant was lit solely by candles. Freesia perfumed the air. About fifty people sat around at tables spread with starched linen table-cloths and napkins. Candles floated in glass bowls. The family ranged in age from about four to eighty. Mario brought Kathleen to the top table to meet his parents. Nessa could feel Kathleen shaking. When Mario introduced Kathleen to his mother, she kissed Kathleen warmly. Kathleen shone with delight and relief.

After a succulent meal of seafood and pastas, they danced. Everyone danced, including the children and the grandparents.

Antonio's family eyed Nessa suspiciously when Antonio danced with her repeatedly.

"Antonio...is an only son, five sisters...he inherited the hotel and everything when his father died," Mario said, watching him dance with Kathleen.

"Lucky old Antonio...." said Nessa.

"Yes, I thought so until now. I wouldn't say lucky any more, terrible responsibility...burden of being the only son.... I am the lucky one, I can choose my own wife."

Was he warning her? Did he see the reaction of Antonio's mother?

"You have chosen very well, you're a very lucky fellow."

"Yes I am," he agreed warmly. "Antonio, Antonio can't...." He shifted with embarrassment.

"It's all right, Mario, I get the message."

"But does he?" he sighed. "The family...."

Antonio was coming over with Kathleen, hand outstretched to Nessa.

The following day, Antonio had arranged to show Nessa the sights, starting with a trip to Neptune's grotto. Word came Antonio was called away on business and would be gone for a few days. He hoped to see her before she left. Nessa got the message loud and clear.

She went instead with Kathleen into Alghero. The narrow cobbled streets, flanked by ancient walls, opened out suddenly into squares and avenues lined with oleander and mimosa trees. They had ice-cream outside one of the little cafes on the shaded side of the square and met up with Mario for lunch. Mario, feeling bad about Antonio, booked a trip to Corsica for the two girls for the next day.

Kathleen was too tired and wouldn't get up when Nessa called her at six o'clock the next morning. So Nessa went alone. A busload of guests from the hotel and apartments were going, including Ben, alias "Jaws." On the bus and ferry "Jaws" latched on to Nessa, who neither wanted to be stuck with him nor be rude to him. After the courier had shown them Napoleon's birthplace and said they could do their own thing for an hour or so, Nessa decided to give "Jaws" the slip.

Hopping out of a side door of the shop, she escaped down a side street and ambled around the leafy boulevards of Ajaccio. She was so busy gawking up at a building that she walked smack into three tall people. O'Shea was one of them, Susan another, and a slightly familiar fair-haired man.

"It's Nessa, isn't it...? Nessa of the bent number plate...?" said the faired-haired man.

She looked at him surprised, then recognised the owner of the Mercedes she'd crashed into the day she followed O'Shea. She couldn't remember his name.

"Yes, hello. I'm sorry, I've forgotten your name."

"Terry Horgan, and hello again," he said.

"Seen any good beds lately?" O'Shea said, tossing Nessa's curls.

What does this patronising bastard think he's doing, Nessa thought furiously. She shook her head violently and stuck her face up at him antagonistically.

"Remove your hand, "she said through gritted teeth.

He smiled good-humouredly at her. Her heart raced madly. She wished he wasn't so bloody attractive.

He patted her head, like he would a dog, deliberately provoking her, before casually returning his hand to his pocket.

Turning to Susan, he said, "We almost shared a four-poster, Nessa and me."

"Almost?" said Terry. "Definitely losing your touch, O'Shea."

"Where was I when this *almost* happened?" Susan said. She laughed an icy tinkle, clearly upset and getting agitated.

"London," O'Shea said.

Nessa raged at the two men's chauvinism and felt sorry for Susan.

"We were bidding against each other for the four-poster at an auction," Nessa said coldly.

Relieved, Susan laced her arm through O'Shea's in a clear hands-off-he's-mine gesture.

"I'm Nessa Walsh, by the way," Nessa smiled at Susan.

"Susan Kelly," the woman said.

"What are you doing here?" O'Shea almost demanded.

"Shoplifting."

Terry and Susan laughed. O'Shea looked at her, hard.

"I'm serious," he said

She grinned. "Following you, of course."

"Again? You seem to be making a habit of it."

Susan was getting alarmed. She looked from one to the other.

"It's a joke...only messing...I didn't follow him now, or then or will I ever in the future."

"You've lost me totally...." Susan said puzzled.

"I went through every Walsh with and without an E in the phone book...." Terry was saying.

"I haven't got a phone."

"That swine wouldn't give me your address...."

"I couldn't, I didn't have it at the time."

"Have you acquired it since?" Susan asked, troubled.

"Yes, we have a mutual acquaintance; Fionn and Nessa are friends."

"Since when...?"

"A month or so...."

"I seem to have missed a lot, lately."

"How about dinner tonight, Nessa?" Terry said.

"Sorry, I can't, I've to catch the ferry."

"You're not staying here in Corsica?"

"No, Sardinia, Alghero, just came across to have a look at the rich. Now I've seen them and know I'm not missing anything, I'm going back to culturally rich Alghero."

"Watch out for the bandits in the hills," said O'Shea.

"Alas, I'm too poor to be of interest to them."

"Bet those lucky Sardinians are queueing up to take you out," said Terry.

"I have been propositioned like everyone else...but unfortunately not by the great Italian lovers, only so far by the lechers, offering themselves as bed companions. But then, the world is full of nasty men offering time share in their beds. You get it everywhere, even at auctions in Ireland."

O'Shea actually coloured. She was thrilled.

Terry hooted, "You've met your match, O'Shea."

"I'm no match for O'Shea... he's the kind my Gran warned me against..."

"A good tutor.... From one who knows." said O'Shea.

"Will you settle for dinner with an ordinary Irish one?" Terry asked.

"Lecher?"

"No, lover, bedless of course...friend, traveller ...acquaintance...anything?"

"Owen," Susan said, "I must be thick or something, but I don't seem to be getting the drift...*you know* Nessa's grandmother?"

Nessa, afraid of the negative account O'Shea would give, jumped in before O'Shea could answer.

"Fionn and my grandmother were...were...."

"Go on, Nessa, tell Susan about Fionn and the divine Deirdre...."

"Deirdre! Not Deirdre the *vamp*...." Susan exclaimed. "The one who legged it when poor Fionn went to England to seek his fortune?"

"Got it in one...." said O'Shea smugly.

"God, Fionn never stops about her," Susan said, "driving us all mad."

"Sorry for your trouble," Nessa said sarcastically.

"Owen," Susan said, ignoring Nessa, "why didn't you tell me Fionn found his Deirdre? He must be over the moon."

"Not exactly," O'Shea said.

"Ah...didn't she have a good enough alibi for leaving him in the lurch?" she sniggered.

"She couldn't," Nessa said shortly.

"I bet she couldn't," Susan said.

Nessa no longer felt sorry for Susan. "My grandmother couldn't defend herself because she was dead...."

That wiped the sneer off Susan's face. Even

O'Shea looked embarrassed.

"And now if you'll excuse me....."

"A drink, Nessa...have a drink with us before you go," Terry almost pleaded.

"We shouldn't keep Nessa, she hasn't much time before the ferry sails," Susan said.

"Thank you, Susan, for your concern, I was going to decline on those grounds anyway."

"We'll walk you to the harbour," O'Shea said firmly.

"No, no thank you, I've a bit of shopping to do. And I've to meet up with our courier."

She spied "Jaws" loitering with intent at a nearby cafe.

"Hey Ben, wait for me!" she shouted.

"See ya...."she said, bolting after the surprised Ben, who could hardly believe his luck. He smiled his wolf smile and tried to buy Nessa coral beads, gold brooch, something...anything. Nessa declined but allowed him buy her an ice-cream....

When Nessa told Kathleen about her meeting with O'Shea et al, and what Susan said about Deirdre leaving Fionn in the lurch, Kathleen was furious, even with Nessa excluding the *vamp* bit.

"The next time I see that O'Shea, I'll, I'll...imagine telling Susan that...pity I wasn't there, I'd, I'd...."

"To be fair, I think it was Fionn who told her about Deirdre, calling her the love of his life."

"Oh I see...but still, bet Fionn didn't put it like that...making her out to be a gold-digger...the cheek of her judging Deirdre without knowing the circumstances."

"Yeah. I wish we knew what happened ...exonerate her."

"Why don't you ask Oisín? If anyone knows, it's Oisín. Deirdre and he were very close...."

"I wrote all right, but haven't posted it yet...I was going to ask you...then events sort of took over.... I'll send it the minute I get back...." she hesitated. "Kay, when you saw Fionn...did he remind you of anyone?"

"To be honest, I didn't look at him very much...and I'm not particularly observant at the best of times...."

"Think."

"Not really...maybe an army colonel...or an actor...let me see...you know that fellow in...?"

"No, no, someone we know."

"Well, on reflection...there was something familiar...his smile...."

"Without the moustache...younger...fairer... Australia...." prompted Nessa.

"Jesus Christ...not Oisín, you're not thinking Oisín?"

"That's exactly who I'm thinking of. I'd nearly swear Oisín is Fionn's son."

"There you go again, jumping to conclusions."

"I really feel sure. There's something about him, apart from his looks. Little mannerisms...."

"Why didn't you tell me?"

"I thought it might be my imagination...I was waiting to see would you see the resemblance and when you said nothing...."

"Ah now, Nessa...the night that was in it.... It was a struggle to look at anyone else but Mario.... Imagine finding your son at eighty-something ...there's hope for me yet...." Kathleen said wistfully. Then all business, "You know what you've got to do?"

"What?"

"Ring Oisín immediately...right now...."

"But Kay—say if I'm wrong?"

"But what if you're right? If Oisín knows he was illegitimate...he'll want more than anything...take it from me...I know, Nessa."

"What'll I say ?"

"Tell him you met Fionn...nothing heavy...tell him what Fionn said about Deirdre...just tell him everything except the likeness...."

Nessa rang.

She didn't know what time it was in Australia. She got the answering machine. She didn't leave a message. Hounded by Kathleen she rang the next morning—already evening in Sydney. The answering machine again. This time she left a message, "Nessa rang to say hello."

"You've got to come," Kathleen said firmly, "It's only a barbecue for Chrissake...."

"What did I say about gooseberrying before we left Ireland?"

"How will you be a gooseberry...everyone from the hotels around will be there, as well as the locals, and Mario's hardly going to throw me flat on my back in the middle of the dance floor, now is he?"

"How would I know?"

"Don't be such a bitch, Nessa, you know well I'm going back to his place after...."

"Yes."

"Look, all I'll be doing at the barbeque is dancing and eating, OK? While I dance with Mario, you'll have plenty of partners, you'll be fighting them off.... Pity about Antonio.... Anyway, I want to go to this barbecue and I'm not going without you, right ?"

"OK, OK, I'd love to go."

The place was dark and mysterious in the middle of a wood, lit only by fairy lights. They ate chicken and all sorts of barbecued things, like peppers and aubergines, and drank quite a lot of wine. The lads were indeed queueing up to dance with Nessa, the madonna with the wild hair.

"Why are they calling me the madonna with the wild hair?" Nessa asked Mario.

"It is different," Mario said, "the colour...the curls ...so much...."

A shaggy dog, or something equally disparaging, was how O'Shea described it. But now here in Sardinia she was the madonna with the wild hair. And she felt wild and wonderful. And giddy from the music and wine. Towards the end of the night when the music had softened and become romantic, O'Shea was at her side.

Mario, surprised and delighted to see him, jumped up, welcoming him to Sardinia, pumping his hand up and down. Encouraged him to sit with them. Kathleen nodded coolly.

"What's wrong with Kathleen?" O'Shea asked as he led Nessa out to dance.

"I told her what a bastard you were."

"Thanks."

"You're welcome."

He held her gently, then closer, protecting her from being crushed. Her body reacted. She looked up at him. He smiled down at her.

She wanted to punish him...lead him on, then

run away. Unfortunately, her body was reacting to his closeness without engaging her brain.

"What are you doing here?" she asked

"Dancing with you."

She stiffened.

"Temper, temper," he said holding her tighter. "I've decided to stay a few days around Sardinia."

"Susan?"

"Assignment in New York."

"Terry?"

"Ah Terry.... Terry is gone to Rome...on a wild goose chase...."

"How do you know?"

"I orchestrated it."

"What does he do?"

"Same as me, collects beautiful things, we're friends, rivals, hunt the same little gems. Same taste. At college together. Know each other too well."

"And you deliberately gave him a bum steer ?"

"Yes. Got a friend to ring him from London, telling him he had seen a piece in Rome that Terry has been seeking for eons," he said happily.

"With friends like that...."

"We do it all the time to each other.... I can read his mind. He has designs on you."

"Oh that's nice, I find him very attractive myself," she lied.

"Suppose he is, I wouldn't know."

"Is that why you did it?"

"No, I would probably have done it anyway. Given the opportunity he'd do exactly the same and has done. He's probably picked up some other little gem or he could be on his way here."

They danced in silence.

"You're very small...."

"You're very pass-remarkable. And what's more I'm almost five four...."

"Almost," he mocked. "Almost twenty-three, almost anything else?"

"Almost in love," she said.

His face showed genuine surprise.

"With whom?"

She smiled enigmatically.

"You'd want to be wary of these beach romeos."

"He's not a beach romeo, he owns the hotel and apartments we're staying at."

She almost laughed, watching the incredulity on his face.

"He's not a lecher either, hasn't asked me to go to bed with him or anything."

"What has he asked?"

"To marry him, actually," she lied.

"Fast worker. How come he let you out alone?"

"I don't have to be let out. I do what I like. Anyway, he knows I wouldn't go with anyone I met at a barbecue. Besides, Mario and Kathleen are chaperoning me."

"You didn't answer my question, where is he?"

"Working."

"So you want to be an old man's darling."

"I didn't say that, anyway he's not that old."

"Fiftyish?"

"Younger than that."

"Forty-something?"

"Younger that that."

"Thirties?"

"Not that old...twenty-five...no six, actually."

Trying not to smile, she watched his face.

"Young to own an hotel."

"Only son and heir."

"What's he like?"

"Magnificent. Puts Michelangelo's David in the shade."

"Really?"

"And he's such a nice person as well. Not a bit pompous or anything."

He was silent.

"He calls me the madonna with the wild hair."

O'Shea cracked up laughing. "The madonna with the wild hair...."

Why in the name of God did she say that? She blamed the wine. But she knew it wasn't.

"Do you think Kathleen would mind if this bastard comes over to the table?" he said full of charm.

"Yeah, she'd mind and if she knew what you thought of Deirdre...see that?" Nessa pointed to an enormous skewer on the grid, "she'd stick it right...."

"OK, I get the message."

The music started again.

"May I...?"

"Why not? At least you're being a nice bastard...well niceish."

He laughed and she laughed. She relaxed and they had great fun trying to dance an oldie like a mambo or something.

"May I leave you home?"

"No, I came with Mario and Kathleen and I'm going back with them."

"How about a swim in the moonlight?"

She looked up at his beautiful face. Please God

protect me from myself. "I...I'm not sure.... No, Kathleen wouldn't approve."

"Would she know?"

"I'd tell her."

The music stopped. The floor cleared. Nessa made to move. O'Shea took her elbow.

"Skewer or no skewer, I'm not standing here. I'm going over anyway."

O'Shea asked Kathleen to dance. Hesitating, she looked at Mario. Mario, misinterpreting, said, "Of course you must dance with Owen."

Nessa watched. Kathleen was stiff in his arms. Hostile. Owen was talking. He danced her over to the skewer and whispered something into her ear. Kathleen turned scarlet. She said something with a deadly serious look. O'Shea said something smiling. Kathleen laughed.

The creep was getting around Kathleen before her very eyes....

When they returned to the table, Kathleen was no longer cool to O'Shea. Nessa felt betrayed. Mario already thought O'Shea was great and now Kathleen was changing her mind. Nessa glared at her. Kathleen didn't look in her direction.

Bet he didn't tell her he called Gran a vamp. She felt sorely tempted. But she didn't. She sulked.

CHAPTER EIGHT

The moon was full. The beach deserted. The water green and clear. Gently lapping. Nessa could hardly breathe. She'd play it cool. Have a swim and go back. No big deal. A moonlight swim. She plaited her hair and clipped it on top of her head.

"Ready?" O'Shea said standing over her in his swimming trunks.

"You go ahead...I'll follow...slowly."

"Snorkel?"

"No thanks."

He hung it around his neck, charged into the sea and swam out to the deep. Cautiously Nessa trod the water on tiptoes. She gave a little yelp when the chilly water washed against her warm stomach as she passed into rougher water. O'Shea stopped swimming.

"You should try the snorkel, Nessa," he shouted to her, holding it up. She shook her head. He put it on and dived under the waves.

After a few breast strokes she lay on her back and began to float.... She shouldn't be here. Looking for trouble. After all she said...and here she was on a moonlit deserted beach with the man she hated...a man she was afraid she didn't hate enough...a man she'd find it hard to say no to....

It wasn't her fault...she argued...it was a case of the devil you know.... After the barbecue, when Kay and Mario left her at the apartment, "Jaws" was on his balcony. At three in the morning! On the balcony! For God's sake! She felt he was waiting for her. His saliva-filled "Good night Nessa," shivered through her whole body. She should never have run after him, taken that ice-cream....

Kathleen, though saying nothing, must have noticed her stiffen because after she and Mario had escorted her up to the apartment they waited outside till Nessa locked and bolted the door. Kathleen called twice from the bottom of the stairs, "Back in an hour, Nessa," for "Jaws"'s big ears.

Nessa had just brushed her teeth when the door bell rang, striking terror into her very soul. She let it ring. Then with her heart walloping off her ribcage she spoke into the intercom.

"Yes?" she said in a cracked voice.

"It's me Nessa, Owen...may I...?"

"Yes, yes," she said with relief and pressed the button opening the main door. He thundered up the stairs. She let him in. And before he had the words out asking her, she was agreeing to go swimming with him. Her eagerness surprised him.

She told him about "Jaws."

"I thought it was my irresistible charm."

"That as well," she said, grinning.

"There are fascinating things to see under the sea," he said holding out a snorkel.

"I know, I've seen it all on film and that's enough for me.... I'm a bit water-phobic...like to keep my head above water...if I think I'm out of my depth, I panic and sink like a brick," she said.

"I'll take care of you, don't worry," he said, locking the door and pocketing the key.

Feeling well out of her depth she went with him gladly.

He surfaced beside her, startling her, knocking her off balance, making her swallow a mouthful of water. Reacting, she pushed his head under. He disappeared ...seconds galloped into minutes... Oh God I've drowned him...don't be silly, he'll come up, he had to...she had come up, three times...the third time grabbed by the hair and hauled out, the time she nearly drowned in the river....

"Owen, Owen," she wailed, puncturing the silent night...not a ripple.... Maybe he hit his head...his lungs filled with water.... "Owen," she whispered, hardly able to breathe.... A swish of water and she was scooped up and carried out to the deep in a spray and a scream.

"I'll teach you, you wild-haired madonna."

She stuck to him like clingfilm.

"I'm sorry, I didn't mean to...."

"Oh yes you did, and you're going to get your comeuppance."

"Please, please, I shouldn't have...it was dangerous...don't don't, I'm a coward.... Look at my back...there's a pure yellow streak running down...a total coward.... If you put me down here I'll drop like a stone to the bottom...and maybe never surface...."

She had his neck in a vice grip, her legs lashed around him.

He looked at her white frightened face.

"OK...OK...anyway, I haven't much choice.... I'd have to break your arms and legs to disentangle you."

He turned and carried her back to the shore. "It's time you were out anyway...."

"Thanks," she said uncoiling. There was a sort of suction plop as her skin pulled off his. He picked up her thin threadbare towel, discarded it and wrapped her in his thick fluffy one.

Giving her a brief rub, he said, "Can't have you catching cold...."

"But what about you...?"

"A run on the strand will do the trick."

Cosily snuggled into the towel, she watched him jogging down the beach. When he returned there were only a few drops of water glistening on his body. He took her flimsy towel and dried his hair. She undid her plait and shook out her hair. He rubbed it with the towel.

"The madonna with the wild hair...."

"Ah shurrup, you spoil everything."

"Honestly Nessa, I wasn't jeering, I really meant it. Your hair is beautiful."

He kissed her hair, then her lips....

She kissed him back...she put her tongue in his mouth, tasting the sea. She burrowed into him. She couldn't stop...passion rising...out of control.

"Nessa," he said.

She opened her eyes....

He held her shoulders. "I don't want to take advantage...I...."

It was as if he'd thrown a bucket of cold water over her...like a bitch in heat.

She drew back into the towel. Ashamed. Pulling her T-shirt and shorts over her wet bikini, she marched off, upbraiding herself.... Why am I so

weak...throwing myself at him...allowing him to
reject.... I'm a stupid stupid cow...and after Howth
...never...never, I said. He turns up in Sardinia and
I offer myself on a plate... proving his opinion...an
easy lay...a vamp...and he says, thanks, but no
thanks...pity he didn't drop me in the deep...drown
me...it would have been so much kinder.

She was so busy whipping herself she didn't
realise she was barefoot till she stood on something
sharp cutting her sole. She watched the blood
pouring out, not caring, and limped across the road
to the apartment. O'Shea, catching up with her,
took her arm. She shook him off...hobbling on.

He followed her to the door.

"Bugger off, "she said.

Ignoring her he took the key from his pocket,
opened the door and went in. She sat down on the
sofa and watched the blood drip on the tiled floor.

"First-aid box?" he asked.

She shrugged. He went to the bathroom and
returned with disinfectant, plasters, bandages and
a bowl of hot water.

"Take those clothes off."

Her two fingers shot up in the air.

"You'll get your death in that wet bikini...." he
said, nodding at the wet patches.

She went into her bedroom leaving a trail of
blood and changed into a long T-shirt and leggings.

"Now for the playing doctor bit," he said. "Bit of
a foot fetish, into feet in a big way."

"Runs in the family."

"I should imagine they do in most families."

Smart arse, she thought but said nothing. She
stuck her foot into the water. The water turned

black from the dust. Gently he washed her whole foot, threw out the water and bathed the wound again in clean water. Pressing her teeth together, she barely flinched when he poured the disinfectant.

"What a brave little thing you are," he said

"Runs in my family. From my maternal grandmother."

He took the bowl and things into the kitchen. She could hear him washing the bowl and putting the stuff back in the presses.

"Tea, coffee?" he said.

She shook her head.

"Right, I'm off."

She didn't answer.

When he went she washed the blood off the floor. Then showered with her foot stuck out through the curtain.

She lay in bed fully awake. Drained. She'd nearly welcome a mugger...one with a large knife to plunge into her heart...if only she and Antonio...so nice... genuinely nice...even rich...and beautiful...far better looking than O'Shea.... A prize catch.... If the family hadn't...would she...? No...she couldn't imagine...even if they welcomed her with open arms. Her heart was lost to that brute O'Shea. She loved him passionately whether she liked him or not. Maybe that's what most people do, love and lose and settle for the safe, the nice, the comfortable. Someone safe like her grandfather. And fantasise about the passionate lover, the one that got away.... Is that what Gran did ?

Fionn said he regretted all his life not having fought for Deirdre "...Owen would have...Owen most definitely would," he said. What was Owen doing...followed her to Sardinia, checking her out, testing her and discovering she didn't measure up...that she wasn't what he wanted...got her out of his system...or maybe he was testing himself...? "Will I be able to resist the temptations of Nessa the Jezebel...or will she have her wicked way with me?"

All very well Doc O'Brien saying you shouldn't close up your heart...but that's exactly what she was going to do. Wrap it in layers so that it couldn't be got at again. It was her only hope of survival. Tomorrow would be their last full day in Sardinia. She wished she was already home, finalising her arrangements to go to Australia.

Oisín...linked with Fionn...and panic...suppose Fionn died before Oisín could.... She'd ring Oisín tomorrow...and tell him.... And for their sake she'd be civil to O'Shea and try to appear friendly.

She got up and walked out on her balcony. It was a beautiful, still night, the flowering trees perfuming the air.... Mid-winter now in beautiful Sydney...the blue mountains and the psychedelic parrots.... Oisín might take Fionn out for a holiday, like he did her grandfather. It was almost incomprehensible to know, or almost know, they weren't father and son. A second father for Oisín...imagine a second father at sixty-odd.... Would he be upset...? Say if he doesn't know...still thinks grandfather.... If only Gran was around.... Her heart pinched with sadness.

"So, you vant to be alone?" Kathleen teased when Nessa refused to go to Fertilia with herself and Mario the next morning.

"Yes, I want to wander around Alghero on my

own."

"Pull the other one," said Kathleen.

Mario said, winking, "If you should *happen* to come across O'Shea, invite him to the going-away dinner."

They looked so happy thinking she had an appointment with O'Shea, she promised to invite him *if* she saw him.

The big *if* cemented their suspicion and sent them off child-happy. She suspected they knew about the rendezvous with O'Shea. Did he tell them his plan for a midnight swim?

The cut, when she examined it, was quite small and had almost closed. But it was very tender, bruising navy right across her foot. She was glad she had her trainers. She put on her white leggings and white T-shirt under a big yellow cotton shirt and negotiated her damaged foot into her cushion-soled trainer. Pain zig-zagged around her foot settling in a slight throb.

The bus into Alghero took only a few minutes. The cobbled streets did nothing for her sore foot and after a short time she was limping. Gazing at the treasures in a little jewellery shop, she lusted after a little coral ring. Having twisted her body and turned her head upside down she read the price tag. Dizzy from the price or being upside down, she reeled up the street.

Anyway, she consoled herself, she had read somewhere coral was becoming an endangered species, so because of her impecuniosity she wouldn't have to worry about compromising herself. She remained ecologically correct. Feeling almost virtuous, she moved on.

She'd love to buy a little present for Fionn. Something small...and Oisín, some little antique...she rationalised if she couldn't pay for a modern thing, an antique was out of the question.... She kept looking at things, counting her money and turning away.

She was as surprised as ever when the dark narrow street opened out into a sunlit square, lined with mimosa and oleander trees. She was lucky to get a seat at a table outside the cafe. She ordered coffee and ice-cream and sat in the shade of a mimosa tree.

God, she thought, what if Mario and Kathleen announce their engagement tonight? They said they had some special shopping to do, looking at each other in the way lovers do, shredding Nessa's heart. She'd have to get a present.... She'd have to use all her money on Kathleen. She'd give Oisín Gran's writing box, the match of Fionn's. He'd like that.... He didn't, wouldn't, take anything at the time...just some photographs.

Refreshed, she counted her money. She had almost a hundred pounds. She'd blow the lot on something old, small but unusual, for Kathleen and Mario.... She could probably borrow a few pounds from Kathleen and get Fionn a bottle in the duty-free.

The antique shop was like nothing she had ever seen before. An Aladdin's cave full of the most exquisite antique china and pottery. Everything she looked at was magnificent. So incredibly beautiful, so richly decorated, so unbelievably expensive.... Amazing china plates, bowls and chargers...names like Castelli, Castel Durante,

Francesco Durantino, Farini, and price tags with thousands of noughts dripping off them.

Twenty-four thousand pounds for a sixteenth-century painted Venetian oviform jar! She converted the money again.... No, she had converted correctly.... Twenty-four thousand pounds.

She fell in love with a magnificent Cantagalli charger attributed to Farini. It worked out at about eight hundred pounds. She was giving up in despair when she saw a little majolica armorial two handed vase prettily painted with a milkmaid, a shepherd and a cow that Kathleen would love.

Nessa did her sums...again converting lire into pounds. It worked out at about one hundred and ninety-eight pounds. It sounded so inexpensive after all the thousands. But it might as well be thousands as far as Nessa was concerned....

She left dejected. She might find something tiny but special in some little second-hand shop or a market. She walked around Alghero in the full midday sun, her foot throbbing, her shirt now sticking to her back through the wet T-shirt. She went into the old church for solace and shade. Her teeth chattered in the sudden chill. "Jaws" was sitting on a bench in the gloom. He looked so vulnerable just sitting there. She felt vulnerable too, and poor as her mind returned to monetary matters. She did her sums again. If she baby-sat for Oisín's rich neighbours when she got to Australia she'd make loadsa money. Easily be able to be independent. Hardly need any money going over.

O'Shea, he was in the trade. He could get her a reduction. Hardly knock two hundred pounds off an item of three hundred pounds, but he might know somewhere inexpensive or she could ask him if she saw him for a loan... But how what would she say to him? "Hi Owen, I was wondering if...." Or she could say, "I'm in a bit of a spot...." She was sure she'd think of something...all she needed to do was meet him.

But she didn't even know where he was staying. Again out in the glare, she made her way to the posh antique shop. She might find some little precious thing in a corner, not valuable at this moment, but in a few years time could become a collector's item...she'd have a little root....

She kept seeing O'Shea everywhere. He can't be that special if half of the tourists in Alghero look like him, she thought. She saw the real O'Shea. Through the window of the antique shop. He had bought something and they were wrapping it in gold and black paper. She felt jealous of his ability to buy in such a place. She pysched herself up...what to say.... She'd come straight out with it.... "I was wondering if you could lend me a few quid...." He emerged. She moved into the shadows and watched him pass.

Moving into another little street, she found a much less exotic antique shop full of little treasures. Unfortunately, most started about two hundred pounds. Two things she fancied were just about in her price range, between ninety-five and ninety-six pounds; a pretty glass vase engraved with celery c1870 and a pair of champagne flutes. Eventually she decided on the vase. They wrapped it in dark green paper, tied gold ribbon around it and gave her a gift card. She held the precious gift to her. Her anxiety evaporated, she felt wonderful. Heading towards to bus-depot she met "Jaws" emerging from the church.

"How about an ice-cream, Ben?" she said. His face lit up.

After the dinner, Mario and Kathleen announced their engagement to cheers and clapping and a roll of drums. Mario wept. As Nessa congratulated Mario and Kathleen, she shyly slipped Kathleen the present. Mario said he loved the celery on the side and Kathleen said it was the nicest present she ever got. Her only antique. Nessa was chuffed.

Nessa shared a table with Antonio and his six minders: the five sisters with their big brown eyes and their sharp little teeth, and his mother. All watching. His mother, friendly, calling her the pretty little schoolteacher. Flashing great big neon smiles at her. Smiles that almost reached her eyes. Antonio in his innocence interpreted their defrosting as a change of heart.

Nessa knew it was her imminent departure that made the mother relax and smile on her. And more than likely she had been told Nessa had a fella.

There was a empty place beside Nessa for him. For O'Shea. She should have told Kathleen and Mario he wouldn't be coming. She had tried but they were so engrossed in their engagement and everything. It wasn't her fault. She nearly didn't see him. And she couldn't be expected to run after him with her sore foot....

O'Shea arrived bearing gifts. Well one gift. It was wrapped in black and gold paper with ribbon. After

congratulating the happy couple, Mario escorted
him to Nessa's table and introduced him to his
aunt and cousins. The five foolish virgins forgot
about protecting Antonio and began flirting with
O'Shea. He reciprocated. Apart from a nod of
acknowledgement when he arrived, Nessa ignored
him. Well, pretended to ignore him. Luckily he was
sitting beside her so she didn't have to look at him.

There were gasps of delight when Kathleen
opened the present. It was the Cantagalli charger
that Nessa had drooled over earlier.

"Fuck you," Nessa said under her breath.

"Did you say something, Nessa?" O'Shea asked.

"No, why?" she looked at him. "Expecting a
round of applause for your charger?"

He definitely blushed. She was glad.

"Heard in Fertilia you were searching Alghero
with a fine toothcomb looking for me," he said.

"What?"

"Seeking me out with the invitation."

"Oh that, I was to ask you *if* I saw you."

"And you didn't."

"Ten out of ten. You have a rare gift of seeing the
obvious."

"Thank you. I do my best."

"What were you doing in Fertilia?"

"I had a mission; Mario said last night they were
going. I presumed you'd tag along gooseberrying,
so I decided I'd take you off their hands."

Pure hate coursed through Nessa's body,
paralysing her.

"But," he continued, "when I got to Fertilia,
they said I had a date with you in Alghero. I
pretended we had and rushed back to save your

face."

Still dumbstruck, she wanted to pulverise him,
hear his bones crack and crumble.

"Sincerely, Nessa, if you wanted to see me why
didn't you ask? I'd have managed to give you an
hour...or at least half." He smiled at her.

"Listen, you," she said. "They asked me to invite
you here tonight when we'd meet. I said we weren't,
but if I saw you I'd pass on the invite, right?
Unfortunately, they didn't believe me."

"The lady doth protest too much syndrome."

"You are truly amazing, as well as being a
wonderful warm human being you have massive
brain power...why don't you take both and shove—"

She was interrupted by shouts of encouragement
as Mario's father got to his feet. He made a speech
welcoming Kathleen to the bosom of his family,
causing a terrible sadness to seep into Nessa's soul.
She'd ring Oisín as soon as she got a chance.

When the dancing commenced, Nessa declined
on account of her foot. Antonio said he'd take her
in his arms and her feet wouldn't have to touch the
floor. She still refused, saying she'd enjoy the
music and watching the dancers. O'Shea danced
with the sisters, all looking up at him with their
beautiful brown eyes. The two youngest, about
sixteen and seventeen, looked as if they were
already smitten, and he smiled down on them
charmingly. Even the aunt forgot about protecting
Antonio when O'Shea asked her to dance. Nessa
had a pain in her jaw trying to keep a smile on her
face. When she could bear it no longer she asked
Mario could she use the phone. Ring Australia.

"No problem...anywhere in the world, Nessa...."

"Nessa?" said Oisín down the line, "What's up pet...are you all right...?"

She was a bit overcome just hearing his kind voice and the words stuck in her throat, she wanted to tell him she was full of grief and jealousy.

"I'm fine, fine," she said, not sounding a bit fine.

"Are you pregnant, Nessa, is that it?"

She laughed. "No honestly, Oisín, nothing's wrong...I'm thinking of going over...would...could I...?"

"Of course, you know you don't even have to ask...you're more than welcome—stay as long as you like...."

"Just till I get an apartment...I'm, I'm... emigrating."

She listened for a pause or an intake of breath. He answered immediately. "That's wonderful Nessa...our little family together on the same continent—but what about Kathleen, is she coming too?"

"I'm afraid not, but she has great news of her own. Kathleen has just become engaged to Mario here in Sardinia and...."

"Hold on a minute, you sound like a foreign correspondent. Talk slowly."

She told him.

"That's great news altogether, could I have a word?"

"Yes...but there's something else...I met this man...."

"You want to bring him with you?" he laughed.

"No Oisín, nothing like that, I'm solo.... An old man...he knew Gran a long time ago...he painted that portrait...you know the one...and is still in love with her...well, with her memory...wants to know everything about her...."

He didn't answer. She could hear him breathing.

"Oisín, Oisín...are...."

"What's his name...?"

"Fionn...he painted the portrait...you know...when Gran was about twenty.... Fionn O'Connor...."

"Say that again, Nessa."

She repeated.

Commotion at the other end...she could hear Oisín yelling, "Alice, Alice, come quick, Nessa has found Fionn O'Connor...." Whoops and screams of joy and a crackled voice broke along the line.

"You've found my father...you've found my father, Nessa...what does he look like?"

"You. You're the spit of him."

He began to cry. Alice took the phone. "Give me your number, Nessa, and we'll ring you back, love."

She gave Alice the number.... If it has that effect on Oisín...what about Fionn, Nessa thought dismally.

Waiting alone in the little office, she wished she'd never stepped into that shop that day.

Alice rang back.

"Nessa, love...sorry, Oisín was so overcome."

"Is he all right...I was afraid I might have killed him."

"He's so happy, it's the best news you could have given him. He wants to talk to you but he's afraid he'll break down...." she laughed. "He's started again, tears of joy, Nessa, tears of joy. Look, love, he's incapable...he says he's going over to

Ireland...there within the week...isn't that right, love?" Nessa heard her ask Oisín. "Sorry Nessa, expect him within the next week."

"I'm leaving Sardinia tomorrow morning."

"Ring when you get to Dublin and reverse the charges and we'll talk then. Give Kathleen our best wishes.... Bye love...."

"Thanks darling," Oisín croaked, "see you soon." And he started to cry again.

She sat for a long time, terrified at what she'd done.

When she returned to the restaurant she was surprised everything was the same as when she left it, everyone dancing.

Antonio was waiting for her. "You give your feet a hard time, first you burn your little toes then you cut your sole," he said escorting her back to her seat. She agreed with him. And now I've got my fingers well and truly burnt too, she thought. She sat with Antonio, watching, but not seeing the dancers stamping up and down until O'Shea came into her line of vision. One of the little sisters was teaching him the tango or he was teaching her. Raw jealousy snipped the corner of her heart and flooded her arteries with pain.

A slow waltz, a really smoochy one, started. She couldn't bear to see O'Shea dancing past with a woman in his arms.

"Dance with me, Antonio," she said.

"Your foot...."

"I can bear it for one dance...." She wanted pure physical pain to sear through her, block out her heartache.

"I will take the weight off your poor foot,

Nessa." And he did, almost carrying her.

When it was all over and goodbyes were in the air, O'Shea said, "Want a lift, Nessa?"

"Sorry...what...?" she said, dragging her mind back from Australia.

"A lift?"

"No thanks, Antonio has already asked, I'm sure one of his little sisters would love one...better still...his mother, nearer your own age group," she said, not able to stop herself.

"I've already asked her, alas her chauffeur is at the door."

"Not your night, is it?"

"Nor yours, I see Antonio's getting into the car with his family...."

"Yes, I declined his offer. I'm going back with Mario and Kathleen, I'm doing gooseberry."

"Whatever you're best at."

Antonio came back and kissed her hands telling her he was hers if she wanted him.

"I'll bear it in mind," Nessa said, hugging him tightly for O'Shea's notice.

"Goodnight, Nessa," O'Shea said, moving away.

She had to tell him about Oisín. Get it over with. Otherwise she'd be awake all night brooding on it.

"Owen," she said steeling herself. "Maybe I'll take that lift after all...if it's still on offer...."

"Yes, please, you were my last hope, as you can see I haven't been able to inveigle anyone else. Of course, I blame the car."

"You would, wouldn't you?"

"Well, it's not my aftershave; six phone numbers were pressed into my hand during goodbyes."

She wanted to say something really clever but she couldn't follow that so she said nothing. O'Shea smiled, triumphant.

"I've something to tell you," she said as they drove out of the town. "My uncle is coming over to Ireland...from Australia.... He'd like to see your grandfather...he knows about the relationship between Fionn and Deirdre...he's very kind...your grandfather would like him."

O'Shea said nothing. Should she tell him everything now? He'll have to know to prepare the old man. She'd no choice...she took a deep breath.

"Oisín thinks Fionn *might* be his father."

He stopped the car, throwing her forward.

"What...your uncle is claiming to be my uncle?"

A little nervous titter escaped from her lips. "I suppose he is."

"Does that make us cousins?"

"No, no relation whatsoever, but it makes Oisín my half-uncle."

"And my half-uncle...it's bizarre."

"I know."

"How long have you had this piece of information?"

"I suspected when I saw Fionn...the resemblance."

"And you never said...?"

"I only thought he *looked* like Oisín...and I had a fever...and I didn't know what to do.... I've been trying to contact my uncle...."

"But you never said anything to me...."

"I didn't have any proof...it was only a suspicion.... And you weren't...I was afraid of you...remember how you reacted?"

"Yes, to my shame."

"But tonight I rang Oisín and told him I'd met the man who painted Gran's portrait, and he said I'd found his father and dissolved in tears."

"If it is true...?"

"He wouldn't want any of Fionn's money or anything—he has plenty."

"Fionn hasn't any money...."

"That's a relief...."

"Fionn...the effect it would have, it might kill him...."

"I know, that's why I told you...."

"Did Deirdre pass him off as the doctor's?"

Nessa's cheeks burned.

"I don't know...they had a fantastic relationship ...my grandfather adored him.... Gran never said a word to me.... Oisín seemingly knew, I don't know how long...."

"But did your grandfather?"

"I honestly don't know."

She kept her eyes fastened on the dashboard.

"Doc O'Brien would help...." she said.

"We'll need all the help we can...I don't even know whether they should meet.... My mother too...she'll have to know."

"OhmyGod, Magda.... You can't tell Magda."

"Don't be ridiculous, of course I'll have to tell Magda, she's part of the equation."

"But she'll ruin everything; Oisín and Alice are gentle sensitive people, they'd need counselling before she's let loose on them."

"You make her sound like a monster."

"With a capital M."

"You're being very offensive; that's my mother

you're talking about."

"I know. Like mother like son."

"Whatever about me, how can you say such things about someone you never even met?"

"It never stopped you pontificating about Deirdre, and I am speaking from first-hand knowledge. I had the unforgettable experience of meeting Magda not once but twice."

"Where? When?"

"In town and in Wicklow. I was in Wicklow, sitting for Magda, the day before I came here."

"You sat for Magda the Monster?"

"Yes."

"Let me get this straight; you met Magda, and, having recognised her as a monster with a capital M, you went down to the woods to her lair.... What does that say for you?"

"Not a lot."

"Pure masochism or pure nosiness?"

Fuck, Nessa thought, I walked straight into that. Nosiness was about right.

"I did it for Fionn actually and at first Magda was sweet asking all about Deirdre. Totally fooled me."

"I doubt that; Magda is strong self-opinionated, silly, self-centred and also big-hearted, very, very kind, and as see-throughable as a pane of glass. Her clothes alone give her away, what was she wearing?"

"Can't remember exactly."

He snorted. "Magda has never gone into town without going to town on her apparel."

"She was colourful...nice...."

"Nice...?"

Why am I lying, thought Nessa.

"Bet she scooped you up, fed and flattered you,

and you were only too glad to sit for her."

"I did it for Fionn," she said defensively. "I even changed my mind but that fellow Rory said Magda would be annoyed with him if I didn't come."

"At what stage did the metamorphosis take place?"

"Sorry?"

"When did she turn from Magda the Nice into a Magda the Monster with a capital M?"

"Soon after I arrived, made me wear stupid clothes, deliberately goaded me. Seemingly that's her ploy so that her painting, are full of angry people glaring out."

"You're telling me you sat for a painter without knowing her style or what she was going to do?"

Nessa didn't answer. She was coming out of this as a prize fool.

"But still you sat, like a good little girl, even when she made you angry?" he teased.

"OK, OK, I'm sorry I said she was a monster, and yes, I am a gullible eejit. I didn't realise she was doing it deliberately. I thought she was just obnoxious."

"I would have given anything to see your face."

"You nearly saw all of me."

"What?"

"I was sitting the day you called."

"If only I'd known."

"You terrified me, prowling outside the bathroom door, trying to get in."

"I didn't know you were in there, I was looking for my mother."

"I know," she said, shaking her head sadly.

"What's that supposed to mean?"

"Nothing, it's none of my business what kind of relationship you have with your mother," she said piously, looking straight ahead in case he'd see through her. "Help is available."

He thumped the steering wheel and with a cry of anguish said, "I'm undone, you've discovered my Oedipus Complex."

Alarmed, she looked at him. He burst out laughing.

"Oh Nessa, you have such a fertile imagination you could plant spuds in it."

Nessa had to smile in spite of herself.

"Look," he said, "this business is too fragile for point-scoring. I'll keep Magda in check. But she does have a right."

"I know, I just wanted to protect my family."

"You've forgotten they're as much mine as yours, and more Magda's than either."

"Don't say that, even if it's true, Oisín's all I've got." Big dollops of tears, without warning, rolled down her face.

"Nessa, Nessa," he said gently.

"Sorry...I am being selfish.... Kathleen says it's the next best thing to Fionn finding Deirdre...."

"How would she...?"

"She's been searching since she was sixteen for her own mother."

"Poor Kathleen...."

"And poor old Fionn," she sniffed.

"Deirdre has a lot to answer for."

"Ah shut up, shut up," she screamed. "We don't know her side of the story. She was good, very good, lovingly looking after all those frightened little pregnant girls...and Kathleen...."

"You're perfectly right, I take it all back and apologise."

She was going to say maybe it was Fionn who abandoned Deirdre but she knew it wasn't true. Poor Gran.

"A trail of pain...." O'Shea sighed.

Nessa was beginning to blame Deirdre for blighting her life too.

O'Shea started the car and drove to the apartment in silence.

"Thanks," she said getting out. "I wish...."

"So do I, Nessa," he said softly and drove off.

She wondered were their wishes the same. She wished they'd never met. It wasn't better to have loved and lost than never to have loved at all.

CHAPTER NINE

After many embarrassingly passionate embraces, Kathleen finally released Mario, boarded the plane and plonked down beside Nessa.

"You nearly made a meal of the poor chap."

"He loved it," Kathleen grinned, her mouth swollen with kisses.

"When's the big day?"

"Two months. Whatever it takes to call the bans, et cetera."

"Ah Kathleen, I can't hang around that long.... Can't you speed it up?"

"Now, Nessa, don't you know I'd marry him tomorrow if I could? What's your problem?"

"I was hoping to go back with Oisín.... I have to get away soon...you know...."

"O'Shea?"

Nessa nodded.

"What's going on or not going on with you and him?" Kathleen demanded. "And what happened your foot...you've already told me two completely different stories...."

"Which one sounds more plausible?"

"Neither...."

"I damaged it running away from O'Shea...."

"He didn't...?"

"No...no...." Nessa almost laughed.

She told Kathleen the painful truth.

"I can't make that fella out. He blows hot and cold. Following you here...then...then *nothing*."

"Yeah, I was beginning to think he was interested...."

"*Interested*...has the hots for you, real bad."

"Till I said yes...."

Kathleen sighed. "There are fellas like that. The excitement of the chase is all.... Give him his due, Owen didn't seem the type...but then I wouldn't know...I usually did the chasing."

"It's paid off handsomely."

"Yes it has, hasn't it?"

She held out her left hand, admiring the cluster of diamonds and rubies. "Pity you and Antonio...we could have made it a double wedding."

"It wouldn't have worked, all those minders."

"All we'd have to do is marry the mother off."

"We should have paired her up with O'Shea, there was a bit of chemistry there. She looked as if she might fancy him."

"Wouldn't anyone? He's not exactly hard on the eye...she's a bit long in the tooth for him though."

"About twelve years, I'd say. If it's all right for a man to be twelve years older than a woman, it should work the other way too."

"I agree totally...mind you, if O'Shea was the new daddy I could see her marrying off all those little girls fast."

"Mmm, the way they looked at him...but I suppose it's more likely to be a Susan-Owen marriage; safe and dull."

"I couldn't live without passion meself," Kathleen said with a faraway look.

"I was just something he had to get out of his system, it seems."

"The creep."

"Yeah."

"I have to confess, Nessa, I feel a bit guilty bad-mouthing him, after all he was so charming and flaithiúlach to Mario and me. He really impressed Mario's family, invited them all over to Ireland...."

"That was just him showing off like his aul wan."

"Maybe so," Kathleen said without conviction. "At least you saved yourself having mad Magda for a mother-in-law."

"Could you imagine?" Nessa shuddered.

She did a take-off of Magda in Grafton Street, making Kathleen shriek with laughter.

"What was she like when you went down?"

"I told you."

"No you didn't, not the real stuff, the nitty gritty.... Was she still attired in her multicoloured dream coat?"

"Sombre black with a grey paint-spattered smock and bare feet."

Digging Nessa, Kathleen said, "See the cloven hoof?"

"Not quite, but she has a bunion trimmed with blue."

"Her blue blood coming through, what?" Kathleen guffawed. "Did you see the toy-boy?"

"Well I'm not one hundred per cent sure, she has this masseur called Rory."

"'Nough said."

"Now I didn't actually see anything, but I heard quite a bit while she was having her massage in the adjoining room."

"Yeah?"

"Squeals and yelps and moans and fits of hysterical laughter."

"The age difference there doesn't seem to matter."

"She offered me Rory's services. I declined, of course."

"Why?"

"I wasn't going to have Rory mauling me."

"Ah, you've no go in ye whatsoever, I've always hankered after a good massage ever since that friend of yours, what's her name…you know the one that went to Kusadasi and had the Turkish bath?"

"Oh, Bernice?"

"Yeah, remember how she described the massage she got from the big Turk?"

"Do I what! She went into every orgasmic detail. I kept imagining her body, fingerprinted from head to toe with Turkish markings, went on about it every day for a month. Eventually I used to run when I'd see her coming."

"The only thing stopping me going to Turkey that year was money."

"And Gran."

"I might have become engaged to a Turk."

"Just as well you didn't, you'd never know whether he loved you for yourself or your passport."

"Do you think it was fate that brought Mario and me together?"

"No, it was that nurse who told you Sardinia was awash with sexy men."

"And wasn't she right.... Mario, my Mario, am I, or am I not, blessed?"

"Yeah, you sure are."

They sat in silence.

"Sorry Nessa, I got a bit carried away with massages, you were saying...?

"No I wasn't."

"Was that it?"

"More or less...except things were really hotting up before I left, getting ready for a party."

"An arty-farty rave-up, no doubt?"

"All I know is, it was starting with a massage and going on from there."

"Jeeesus! A gang massage, what a way to get a party going."

"Yeah, and what could follow that—hardly a prayer meeting."

"An orgy with a capital O, more like."

"Great to be a fly on the wall."

"I'd rather be in the thick of it myself."

"You would, wouldn't you?"

"What's that supposed to mean?"

"You're more into parties, a regular song and dance girl."

"You're pretty good on the hoof yourself." She started to lah-lah a jig. "Remember the medals we won at feiseanna?"

"And when we didn't win, Gran said we were robbed."

They laughed.

"To tell the truth, the real reason I left was O'Shea. I was afraid he'd come back. I couldn't bear to see him, especially if Susan was with him, and as they'd be going my way I'd have to take a lift with them. I felt too vulnerable...you know, after Howth."

"Ah, ye poor aul thing, first Howth and now Sardinia," Kathleen said, hugging her.

"Just as well it happened here...at least he won't be following me to Australia to discover he doesn't want me."

Nessa's voice had a hairline crack in it. Kathleen's blood began to boil.

"If that bugger causes you any more grief, Nessa, leave him to me, I know where to get a bloody great skewer."

Nessa giggled half-heartedly.

Nessa, dozing between sleep and wake, heard a soft wind in her ear carrying words of a song, "If you go down the woods today you're sure of a big surprise, for every...." Her eyes flew open as a warm hand took hers. O'Shea. He smiled at her.

"Kathleen?" she inquired.

"Gone to freshen up."

"What are you doing here?"

"Sitting, singing into your shell-like...."

"Don't be so bloody facetious," she snatched her hand back.

"We are touchy."

"Where's your seat?"

"Back there," pointing vaguely.

How far back, she wanted to know, but was afraid to ask. What had she said...? Her mind raced; Magda daisy-chained to Rory to Fionn to O'Shea to Susan.... She'd said everything, every bloody thing including...ohmygod.... Nessa examined his face for signs of omniscience. There were none. He smiled. That charming enigmatic smile. She relaxed a bit. Anyway, what did she care, it was his own fault if he was eavesdropping. Still unable to ask how far back, she curled her lip as nonchalantly as she could muster.

"About Fionn," he said. "I'll tell him about Oisín coming over...drop his age into the conversation. Fionn knows the day, the hour, he left Deirdre, so he'll know if it's a possibility.... Oisín son of Fionn, like the old Fíanna."

"Fionn said exactly the same thing when I said Oisín's name...he was also interested to know Oisín is an architect...."

"He suspects...hopes maybe...."

"Everyone gaining by wholes or halves ...everyone except me."

"What do you mean?"

"Well, Fionn is gaining a whole son and a few grandchildren, Oisín is gaining a whole father and two halves, Magda a half-brother and whatever, and you a half-uncle and half-cousins."

"All those half-measures."

"It just goes to show I should never do anything by half."

He gave a great barrel of a laugh. She laughed too, but not as well. She was losing part of her uncle Oisín and it mattered.

She looked into his eyes and saw kindness. She looked away again as quickly as possible.

"About the other night, Nessa...."

"Don't...I want to forget it ever happened.... Let's sort out this Oisín and Fionn thing...it's so delicate...we can't afford an argument or a falling out...and we have a habit of rubbing each other up the wrong way.... I don't want anything on my conscience...I'm worried enough about the effect on Fionn...if anything happens to him I'd blame myself."

"I've thought about that aspect of it over and over.... Fionn could die tomorrow from old age or whatever. Of course this will have an effect, bound to...but knowing how he feels...we have no right not to tell him, no matter what the consequences.... If he did die from the excitement, having found a son, Deirdre's and his son, would it be a bad way to go?"

"I suppose not."

"We'll do everything to ease it...maybe you could visit him and tell him Oisín is coming...take it in stages...."

"And Magda...you'll have to keep her under control; she could swamp them, destroy them."

"Cut the crap Nessa, she's not a mad dog or..."

"She'll frighten the life out of Alice, Oisín's wife, I know...."

"Bullshit, Magda's larger than life but great fun. They'll love her. Brilliant at entertaining. If you'd stayed the night of the party you'd have seen her in action."

He laughed.

"The massages...absolutely hilarious. They were so shy at first, all huddled together. Nobody willing to take the plunge...."

She could feel her mouth pleating in disapproval.

"Did the weather hold up?" she said to stop him elaborating.

"Yes, it was so good they had their massage in

the herb garden."

"Out in the open?"

"Well, it's a walled garden, a suntrap, perfect setting...and once the first bit of flesh was exposed, they lost their inhibitions. Within seconds they were all at it, comparing lumps and bumps, like war wounds. Jeering each other and laughing at themselves while they waited their turn. The craic was mighty."

"Fionn was part of all that?"

"The instigator, got the whole thing going, slowly unlacing his shoe then, snail-like, inching off his sock, till lily-white flesh appeared to a mighty cheer, *and* it was also his idea to organise a competition for the ugliest pair, the most—"

Nessa interrupted. "That's absolutely gross, I'm surprised at Fionn."

"Ah come on Nessa, loosen up, what's gross about a pair of old carbuncled and bunioned feet still functioning?"

"Feet?"

"What else would have bunions on them? Pat and Rory said in all their time massaging feet they had never seen so many notches and...."

"All these people were having foot massages?"

"In the capable hands of Pat and Rory...you met Pat, Rory's wife?"

She shook her head.

"Rory is good, but Pat has the gift, a heaven-sent reflexologist."

"Reflexologist?"

"Same as Rory, didn't he do your feet?"

"No."

"I thought Magda always engaged him to attend

to her sitters."

"She offered all right but I refused...can't stand anyone touching my feet...giddy, you know?"

"Really? From what I recall, I would have said you weren't in the least bit ticklish, unlike Magda—she squeals and yelps even with Pat. You must have heard her roaring."

"I may have heard a little tinkle."

"She only lets Rory do her feet if Pat's not around."

Now full sure he had heard everything she said about his mother and Rory, Nessa in panic closed her eyes and prayed he hadn't.

"Are you all right, have you a problem with reflexology?"

"Know nothing about it. Barely know the terminology."

Trying to divert him, she said, "Why were all those old people having their feet massaged, were they sitting for Magda?"

"No. Dancing."

"Ballroom?"

"Set-dancing; Magda and Fionn are into it in a big way and the local old folks' club agreed to teach them, so Magda engaged two accordion players and arranged for a busload of over-sixties to come to her place. You should have seen them stepping it out. They were massive. They taught me a thing or two."

He paused. She could think of nothing to say.

"Rory and Pat laid on a mouth-watering meal, much appreciated...."

"I can imagine, I sampled his food at lunch, it was truly scrumptious," Nessa said.

"When my father was asked in a television interview recently what he missed most apart from Magda, he said Pat's nimble fingers and Rory's food."

Shit, she thought, I'm in deep shit and he's rubbing my nose in it.

"Yes indeed," he continued, clearly enjoying spelling it out to her. "It was a great night, simple pleasures. The seventy-nine year old lady, who got a bottle of brandy for her *gross* bunioned and carbuncled feet, said she was thinking of having them photographed and Magda said she'd do better than that—she'd immortalise them on canvas."

"That's nice," Nessa said, thinking, I'll never ever say a word about anyone again except in the middle of a field. She wished he'd go away or Kathleen would come back. Her second wish was granted.

"Well, would you look what the wind blew in...? I hope it's not an ill-wind," Kathleen said, looking down on O'Shea menacingly.

"Ah, Kathleen," O'Shea said with that certain smile.

"Don't move," Kathleen said.

"I insist," he said getting up. "Your seat, Kathleen."

"Thank you, do I detect a sudden rise in temperature?" she said sitting down, melting under his gaze..

"You could say that...." O'Shea said, leaning over her.

"Good, hope it's maintained. I hate sudden blasts of ice, makes the vulnerable shrivel up and die."

Nessa was dying all right, with embarrassment. She tried in vain to get Kathleen's attention.

"Things are hotting up all right, I like a nice even temperature myself. Since we left Alghero I noticed a fair bit of turbulence. I was conscious of a lot of hot air rising. In that sort of atmosphere things get out of focus, distorted, know what I mean?" O'Shea asked, looking straight at Kathleen.

"No, haven't a clue," Kathleen said.

Digging Kathleen fiercely, Nessa said, "Imagine, Kathleen, Owen has been sitting directly behind us all the time."

"Right behind Nessa, actually," confirmed O'Shea, smiling.

Kathleen's mouth dropped. Her face flamed.

Giving a theatrical shudder, O'Shea said, "Brrr... do you feel that sudden chill? Hope it doesn't last. I hate when it blows hot and cold...makes me think of *orgies* and *skewers* for some odd reason...."

He returned to his seat.

Nessa reached over and gently closed Kathleen's gaping mouth while putting a finger to her own lips. Then she raped her bag for a piece of paper and a biro. On the back of a picture card of Alghero she scribbled *Don't ask.*

Kathleen took the biro. *I'm asking*, she wrote.

Nessa wrote wildly. *No orgy. No toy-boy. No hanky-panky.*

What then??? Kathleen penned.

Old age pensioners, foot massages and ceilí dancing, scrawled Nessa.

Kathleen's eyes hula-hooped over the seat, then shaking with merriment she stuck her head into her cardigan to stifle the laughs. Nessa pinched

Kathleen severely, only making her snuffle with titters. Nessa was sorry. Really, really sorry for herself.

Every now and then she heard a throaty chuckle from the seat behind.

CHAPTER TEN

When she got back, there was a letter from the solicitor finalising everything. Plus a cheque for one hundred pounds and eighty-six pence. Nessa realised Gran's estate would have been in debt had O'Shea not paid the inflated price for the bed. A flash of guilt, then a flash of memory obliterated the guilt...the magnificent charger; O'Shea could well afford it. Anyway, she didn't do it intentionally. He could have asked for his money back at the time, probably still could. Maybe she should offer him.... No, leave things.

As you see Nessa, Mr Curran wrote, *everything has been taken care of. As to the matter concerning your uncle Oisín, I presume you've read the letter and everything is clarified.*

Nessa borrowed Kathleen's bike, as her own was punctured, and rode down to the local telephone box and rang Mr Curran. He said Gran told him she left a letter for her and one for Kathleen in the writing box.

Nessa cycled home, threw the bike in the hall and raced up the stairs. She opened the box. Carefully sifting, she found only what she'd found before: her own birth cert, her baptism cert, her parents' marriage cert, her vaccination records and

her school reports. She pulled up the bottom layer.
Nothing.

She remembered the secret drawer in Fionn's
box. She felt around for a switch or trigger...she
touched something and it sprang open. There were
two letters: one addressed to her, the other to
Kathleen, and a photo of Deirdre and Fionn
together.

They looked so deliriously happy, so much in
love. A tamer version of Mario and Kathleen.

And the letter. Her hands quivered as she opened
the envelope addressed to her in Gran's spidery
handwriting.

As well as a letter there was something wrapped
in tissue paper. It was a diamond and ruby ring.
Gran's engagement ring.

She put it on her finger and opened out the
pages.

Dearest Nessa,

*There's something I want to tell you. It concerns
your uncle Oisín. Your grandfather is not Oisín's father.
Oisín's father is a man called Fionn O'Connor, the man
in the photograph. A man I loved very much. We were
engaged to be married. The night before Fionn left for
England we made love for the first and last time. I never
heard from him or saw him again.*

*He had promised he'd write every day. Three weeks
passed and I began to get sick in the mornings. I was
both physically sick and sick with worry. I was pregnant.
No word from Fionn. I made excuses, too soon, not
settled in yet and lots of others. When my mother
realised my plight she packed me off to Mayo with slut,
harlot and strumpet, ringing in my ears, to my aunt,*

Nessa. (You are called after her by the way.) I was to have the baby and it was to be put up for adoption immediately. Nobody would know of my disgrace. Not even my father. Mother told him I was ill and needed to go to the country. I was too ashamed to tell him myself. Aunt Nessa was very kind.

I wrote home twice a week asking if there was any word...any word at all from Fionn. Maura, my sister, wrote back saying there was nothing from the rake. I couldn't believe Fionn abandoned me, so I thought he must be ill. Maybe had an accident. Lying somewhere in hospital. Loss of memory. I convinced myself that was it.

One day a letter would come explaining all.

Nothing came except the baby.

I had complications, so the midwife called a doctor. Your grandfather. Sean was the kindest person I ever met. I wanted to die. He coaxed and bullied me.

"Do you want your son, Fionn's son, brought up in an orphanage?" he'd ask when I was particularly down.

I got better for Oisín's sake. I refused to give him up for adoption, backed by Aunt Nessa who defied mother and Maura, saying I could stay with her for as long as I liked. And she'd help bring up Oisín. Mother said I was never to darken her door again. I didn't.

Nessa said Fionn didn't sound like the kind of man who'd abandon his fiancée. And the baby wasn't an issue as he didn't know I was even pregnant. She encouraged me to write to his brother in Dublin whom I'd met on a couple of occasions.

I wrote asking him about Fionn. His landlady wrote back saying said he had gone back to Kerry. I wrote to his home and the letter came back. The whole family had emigrated to Canada. No forwarding address. I *would have committed suicide only for Oisín. The doctor kept dropping in to see how we were. Bringing the odd toy for the baby and little presents for me. Then he began bringing the three of us out for picnics.*

When Oisín was two years old I married him. I loved him dearly if not passionately. A gentle, loving relationship. I know he loved me more than I loved him, but I think I made him happy. No, I know I made him happy. He told me often.

Not long after your mother was born, I saw my father's death notice in the paper. By this time we had moved to Ballsbridge. Sean's uncle, also a doctor, and a bachelor, had died leaving his practice to Sean along with his house. We were well-off. I had lovely clothes. Sean was always buying me things.

I said nothing, not even to Aunt Nessa (who had come up from Mayo to be with me at the birth) and took a taxi to the funeral.

I was wearing this sumptuous mink coat, looking very prosperous. (I know, I know...I was that dumb person who didn't think of the poor animals. At that time nobody did, unfortunately.) Not wanting to be with them, I sat at the back of the church and stood apart in the graveyard. Maura spotted me, and herself and my mother sidled up to me, actually fawning over me, almost reverently touching my mink coat. Smiling ingratiatingly at me.

My prosperity was all due to mother and herself, Maura was saying. Only for them I'd be living in a garret with that down-and-out artist. And boasting how she had put a stop to his gallop by intercepting the cards in the first few weeks and later returning the letters.

Dazed, I listened to her describing my beloved Fionn

arriving on the doorstep like a tramp with his long dirty hair, making a spectacle of himself ranting and raving...shouting, "Give me back my Deirdre." Witnessed by the whole neighbourhood. Making a holy show of them. And how they sent for the police to take him away.

I couldn't believe my ears. These two, my mother and sister, my own flesh and blood, standing there telling how they had destroyed my lover and expecting me to be grateful. I spat in their faces. It was a dreadful thing to do Nessa, but I never regretted it. Watching the spittle run down their startled faces in front of the whole neighbourhood was the best bit.

I marched out of that graveyard. Pride holding me up. I couldn't, wouldn't, let them see....

I broke down when I got home. Understandably Sean was very upset I hadn't told him about my father's death. I explained because of the estrangement I wanted to go alone. Just stay at the back of the church, pay my last respects. He said he understood but was sorry he wasn't at the funeral to take care of me. Such a good man.

The real reason I didn't tell him was because he was such a forgiving man I was afraid he might try to reconcile my family and me. They'd have been all for it because of my new status. And I didn't want that. If I was still unmarried with a child they'd have scorned me.

In the circumstances it was the right decision, albeit for the wrong reason. I was glad Nessa I had saved Sean that extra grief.

The rest of the week was a blur. I couldn't eat or sleep. Only for Aunt Nessa I wouldn't have survived. We talked about nothing but Fionn...well, I talked, she listened. She knew him almost as well as I did. She had heard it all before, of course, in Mayo. But she let me go on and on till there was nothing else to say.

Sean thought I was grieving for my father. I let him. Aunt Nessa came to live with us soon after. I felt privileged to be able to take care of her in her old age as she had looked after me in my hour of need.

I was always waiting, expecting Fionn to walk into my life again. When Sean died I scoured Kerry for any trace of him. Oisín employed private detectives to search Canada, but to no avail.

I wanted him to know I never stopped loving him. To tell him he had a son and why I married. I couldn't bear the thought of him being bitter, hating me. And I wanted him to know Oisín. Oisín, of course, knew from the beginning that Sean wasn't his father. I think it made him love Sean all the more.

Sean was the kindest man in the world and, as I've said, a loving father to Oisín and Niamh and a loving grandfather, as you know, to you, Nessa and Kathleen.

The above information is for Kathleen too. Better if she reads it before her own.

You brought us great joy after the tragedy of your mother's death.

Don't grieve for me Nessa, I had a very happy life. I loved and was loved by two wonderful men. One day I hope you fall in love with a man like either Sean or Fionn and it's reciprocated.

My only regret was not being able to tell Fionn.

Love, Gran.

PS, I enclose the engagement ring your beloved grandfather gave me.

Nessa ran down to Kathleen clutching both letters.

Unable to speak, she pushed the opened letter into Kathleen's hand first. She read, bawling her eyes out, accompanied by Nessa. Then she opened her own letter.

Dearest Kathleen,

I presume you have read my letter to Nessa, so you see families are not all they are cracked up to be.

Sean and I were lucky in our two families; our first, Oisín and Niamh, our second, Nessa and you.

We felt you were as much our own as our beloved Nessa. I go happily to my grave knowing you and Nessa have each other. Sisters. Not blood sisters—but does it matter?

Look at my sister and mother; mean-spirited, sad people. Who'd want to be related to them?

I might have been forced to give up Oisín, like your mother you, but for my dearest Sean and my aunt Nessa.

I hope you meet a loving man and settle down and have children. You have so much to give.

Love Gran.

PS, Your ring is the one my lover Fionn gave me.

The two of them held each other and howled. Then looking at each other's red eyes and noses, started to laugh. Almost hysterically.
O'Shea. O'Shea had to see this letter. Nessa wanted to rub his nose in it. Have him beg forgiveness for his vicious remarks about Gran. She wanted to scream at him, even more because of her own guilt. Yesterday, she herself was blaming Gran for her own predicament.

And Fionn. If she and Kathleen were upset

reading about Gran's plight—what would it do to Fionn? She'd have to see O'Shea immediately. And ring Oisín as well, see when he was coming.

She wished she had her car—drive over to O'Shea's, screech to a stop outside his place, burst through the door, thrust the letter into his face and shout, "Read that, O'Shea."

On second thoughts, maybe it was just as well she hadn't a car. She could just see herself roaring through Rathmines followed by the siren of a police car. Arrested as she pulled up outside the antique shop. Witnessed by a grinning O'Shea.

Pedal power. Once more into the saddle, she rode to the phone box. She rang the antique shop. No answer. She rang Howth...her heart floating at her knees. Eventually O'Shea's voice, clipped, precise on an answering machine. She always felt like an eejit talking to a machine. Did her voice sound as squeaky as it did in her own ears? She took a deep breath and after the pips said, "This is Nessa Walsh. I have some information regarding Fionn and Deirdre. Call in as soon as possible."

She rang Australia. A sleepy Oisín answered.... It was midnight in Sydney. He was coming in two days. Gave her his flight number. He'd get a taxi.... And was cut off. She cycled home.

Kathleen was in her uniform on her way out to work when she got back.

Nessa handed over the bike.

"All you need is a few bells on your toes, Kathleen," Nessa shouted after the radiant golden tanned woman, as she pedalled off in the sunshine, sporting her new rings on her fingers.

She rang her bell in reply.

Nervous, hyper, Nessa wanted to do something. She couldn't just sit there doing nothing with the contents of that letter needing to be told. She wanted to avenge her gran. She'd mend her puncture and cycle over to the shop. He might just be there. Even if he wasn't, it would fill in the time.

Carefully, she put the letter in the pocket of her jeans and rode over to Rathmines.

No jeep. No sign of life. She left a note on the door to contact her urgently. Pedalling home in a sweat, she realised it was still July. Didn't he say he closed the shop for the month of July? Shit. Anyway, he'd get the message in Howth. If he didn't call this evening, she'd cycle out there. No, she thought as she puffed up the hill, her foot beginning to ache, she'd get a taxi to Howth first thing in the morning.... No, she'd go tonight; if he hadn't come by nine o'clock she'd go to him.... She couldn't wait.

Pushing the bike through the gate she saw a pair of gold sandals balanced like scales on either side of the knocker. As she got closer she saw they were hanging from a skewer. She lifted the knocker and they tumbled into her hand.

She gave a grudging smile. The bastard thinks he's so smart, holding the skewer over her. Well, she had a better weapon...the letter...that would cut him to the quick. She looked forward to showing it to him...monitoring his expression...make him eat his words...watch him squirm...he'd be sorry he put that skewer on the door.

Pity she missed him. Would have been nice to come up behind him as he balanced the sandals.

She would have smiled at him coyly and invited
him into her parlour and maybe even apologise
...then hand him the letter. It would have been
perfect....

She dithered. She wanted to follow him out to
Howth that very minute in a red glow of revenge
but her stomach gurgled hungrily. She was so
nervy she had forgotten to eat and now felt
ravenous. The only food in the flat was a black-
skinned banana that had been there before she left
for Sardinia. She savaged it. It was extra sweet, on
the turn. Gave her enough energy to get to the
corner shop for supplies of bread, butter, milk,
eggs, beans and two apples.

After a boiled egg, tea and toast she felt better.
She'd wait till nine as she'd originally planned.
Better if he came here. More in control on her own
territory. Be prepared. She washed the few dishes,
tidied up the place. If O'Shea turned up tonight he
could bring Susan along. She hoped he would. Two
for the price of one. That cow calling Gran a vamp.
She looked at the place through Susan's eyes and
dusted the furniture, even the bits under things,
and tidied the bookcase. She'd shower. Dress
carefully, put her hair up. Look cool...offer them a
drink...she hadn't any...she could run out to the
off-licence.... No she'd give them nothing. Except
the letter. Plenty of food for thought there. Watch
them digest it.

It was only five o'clock and she was totally
agitated, couldn't relax. Pamper herself with a long
slow bath...that's what she'd do...ease her foot as
well.

Lying in the bath, up to her chin in glorious

bubbles, she thought about Australia...getting away from O'Shea...the other side of the world...but even if she never saw him again she'd keep hearing about him now that Oisín is his half-uncle. And Fionn coming on visits showing photographs of the wedding.... Susan the perfect bride, flawless ...splashed across all the newspapers. Impressing her cousins, their cousins, in Australia.

Bizarre! Isn't that what O'Shea said...? And it was. She felt hard done by...everyone gaining and she losing half her uncle, and to whom?

That bastard O'Shea of all people...life was bloody unfair.

At least Gran would have been pleased, that was something.... Oisín and Fionn united...and all her doing, even if it was a fluke. And the letter, she'd exit triumphantly. O'Shea apologising.

The doorbell rang.

O'Shea? No, been already, only half-five... couldn't possibly...definitely not. Mario...or Kathleen. Another blast. She didn't want to move.... Half-five.... Maybe Antonio doing a Mario.... She blushed at the thought...it would be lovely, romantic, but it wasn't what she really wanted...or did she...? Even with his mother out of the way, as Kathleen said.... No she couldn't see Antonio.... A long belligerent blast.... Who'd call in the afternoon...? She ruled out everyone except Danny. It could very well be Danny...she wanted to see him...say goodbye. Might be her only opportunity .... She hauled herself out of her cocoon of bubbles, wrapped the bath sheet securely around her, ran down the stairs and opened the door.

O'Shea stood there.

"Close your mouth Nessa, you did say it was urgent...."

"Yes, but...how did you get here so fast?"

"I was met at the gate on my arrival home by my mother, who hooshed me back into the jeep and told me you wanted me urgently, said there was a message on the machine...."

"Magda!"

"Herself and Fionn are staying with me. Fionn's shopping for new gear." He grinned. "Getting ready to meet his son."

"You told him?"

"Yes I told him. He's elated...got his hair cut...all the works.... Magda wanted him to get a snazzier jacket, but he decided a navy blazer would impress and a silk cravat...no stopping him...and my mother's as bad."

"All's well that ends well," Nessa laughed.

The towel uncurled...leaving her like Eve without her leaves. He stared.

She blushed.

They both dived for the towel and bumped heads. He got it. Handing it to her, his hand brushed her nipple sending shock waves through her system.

"Nessa Walsh," he whispered, "you'll get your death of cold."

He scooped her up, wrapping her in his body and raced upstairs. Giggles pealed out of her. She couldn't stop. He carried her to the bedroom and placed her gently on the bed.

"The madonna with the wild hair," he said half smiling, freeing her hair from the elastic band.

Immediately she reacted. He stopped the words

coming with a tender kiss. Then he kissed her passionately. She responded with vigour. Desire, lust, coursed through her veins. The buttons on his shirt popped as she ripped it open. He kissed her all over starting at her toes and ending at her lips. She wanted to do the same to him but was too shy.

"Nessa," he said, "I...."

She instantly withdrew, remembering Alghero.

"Are you...are you on the pill?"

"No."

"You might regret...?"

She thought of Deirdre.

"I have protection...." he said.

She nodded. Fascinated, she watched him putting on a condom. Apart from now, the only time she'd seen one out of its packet was on a cucumber at a "how-to" demonstration.

She began to titter.

He shot her a hard glance. She told him about the cucumber. Relieved, he laughed and began kissing her softly, then intensely. The heat of his body against hers made her feel erotically possessed.

"Don't be afraid," he said, misinterpreting the panic he saw in her eyes. It wasn't him she was afraid of, but her own out-of-control feelings. She burrowed into him. He entered her gently and with her very first orgasm she absolved him of all his wrong doings and faults....

Kathleen was right, she thought dreamily, there's a lot to be said for passion.

"About Sardinia," he said as she nestled into him under the duvet.

"You hurt me deeply...madly in love with you...I wanted you with my whole body and soul and you rejected me."

"I felt the same way."

"Then what was the problem?"

"I had no condoms."

"Why didn't you say?"

"Before I could open my mouth you were marching off in high dudgeon."

She remembered why he was here.

"I've something to show you."

"Nothing could follow that.... My cup runneth over with love."

"Love?"

"Smitten from that first Tuesday in June, the day of the auction. Do you remember the first thing I said to you?"

"If you want the bed that badly, you'll have to come home and share it with me."

"The offer is still open."

"You, me and the client?"

"Just you and me. I kept it for us."

"Very sure of yourself, weren't you?"

"Sure you were the only woman for me."

"And your client?"

"Got another bed for her. She was looking for any four-poster at a reasonable price. This one is special to us."

"I was meaning to give you some money back...not really ethical, bidding...."

"If you hadn't we wouldn't have met—cheap at any price...."

"Not afraid of sleeping in Deirdre's bed?"

"No, I've forgiven her."

"You've forgiven her?"

"Yeah, I'm all heart."

"You have nothing to forgive her for, it's you who needs her forgiveness, in fact I wouldn't be surprised if she haunts you."

"I'll take that risk. Marry me, Nessa Walsh."

"What about Susan?"

"Ah yes, Susan...I told her. She said she guessed; the way I looked at you in Corsica."

"Did she mind?"

"Well, she said she hoped you'd turn into the burning bush amongst other things."

"Burning bush, what does she mean?"

"Well, your portrait...it's a biblical scene; Moses and the burning bush. You're the burning bush."

"I'm what?"

"The burning bush...a sort of metamorphosis."

"Like a mutant...?"

"More half-woman half-bush."

"Am I recognisable?" she said, her voice high and thin.

"Absolutely, your hair is massive, a real burning bush...mouth a wee bit sour, turned down like when you're in a sulk, eyes blazing but your nose is best."

"What do you mean *best*?"

"Strong."

"Oh God, I'm not hearing this...why did I do it...?"

"Calm down, Nessa, it's wonderful. I'd say Magda's best. She favours the carbuncled feet. Her agent agrees with me, without a shadow of a doubt he said—the burning bush by a nose."

Nessa let out an ear-piercing scream, culminating in a whimper.

Owen shook her gently. "Nessa, Nessa, I was

only messing, winding you up. Magda said you had a thing about your nose, and...."

Nessa stopped whimpering, shook off his grip and turned eyes of flint on him.

"It was a joke...the emphasis is on your hair and eyes...it's magic."

"You, you bastard, you bloody bastard...."

"I'm sorry, really I am," he said, cuddling her stiff body. "And you're right, dead right, I must be. You're the second person to call me that recently, Susan—"

Nessa interrupted, "What else did she say about me?"

"Said you'd probably turn out like Deirdre."

"What's wrong with that?" she demanded.

"Nothing, a woman who could keep a man loving her passionately for sixty-odd years must be very special."

"She was that all right. But I'm not like her in temperament and you're not like Fionn, we would definitely have a very stormy relationship."

"Susan predicts, hopes, one day, sooner rather than later, you'll cut the balls off me...."

Nessa laughed. "She's probably right."

"I'll risk it."

"Will you now?"

"I'll love you, Nessa till the day I die, and I would have followed you to Australia or wherever...to the ends of the earth. Marry me?"

"The risks...."

"I know."

"And I'm not giving up my job."

"You haven't got a job...."

"I mean when I get one I'm not giving it up...I'm

not into domesticity."

A smile almost burst through his lips. He stopped it forming, watching her earnest face. "I wouldn't allow you...." he started

"Allow!" she shrieked. "You can't stop or allow me do anything, I'm my own person...I...I...."

"Will you bloody well let me finish? What I was trying to say was, I wouldn't expect you to clean the house, my cleaning lady is fine, does a proper job."

"What's that supposed to mean?"

"She cleans under and over things," he said, deliberately eyeing the insects gathered in cobwebs at the edge of the window-sill. "Everywhere," he added.

"So I'm not good enough to be your skivvy."

He sighed. "I give up."

A long silence.

"I can't cook either," she said belligerently, the words trembling on her lips.

"Who cares?"

"Are you trying to get at me?"

"Just trying to tell you I love and want you for yourself and not for your domestic or culinary skills."

"That's all right then...but who'd do the cooking?"

"I will."

She glared at him.

"Yes, I can cook...." he answered the unasked question.

"Who cooked the meal that night in Howth?" she demanded.

"I'm not prepared to answer that on the grounds

it might incriminate me."

"Did you?"

"Depends on whether it's a black mark against me."

"You did...ohmygod, you can do everything.... You're too good to be true."

"I can't knit or sew or mend a fuse...and what about my bad temper and my jumping to conclusions and my chauvinism...."

"I'd forgotten for a minute what a nasty bit of work you are. That's all right then, you're anything but perfect. OK, I will," she said sweetly.

"You will what?"

"Marry you."

"You will?"

"Of course, you'll have to curb your bad temper and your chauvinism."

He grabbed her, kissing her long and slow.

"Have you forgotten I've something to show you?"

"I thought you inveigled me here to have your way with me."

"I wanted to punish you."

"Anytime...anytime."

"I mean *really* hurt you, make you feel really small. And maybe kick you on the way out."

"Thanks very much."

"Well that's the way it would have been, only you got your timing wrong."

"I wouldn't say that."

"Anyway, you did my gran a great injustice and I wanted my pound of flesh."

"You can have it, blood and all."

"Be serious."

"I'm all yours...body and soul...get the skewer."

"Stop messing."

She got up, wrapping her robe around her.

"Read that," she said, handing the letter to him. "It's a letter from Gran. It explains everything."

"Are you sure this beast should read a letter from your beloved Gran? I feel I haven't the right."

"You haven't, that's why you must. I'll make us something to eat. I do a wondrous beans on toast," she said defiantly.

"My favourite."

She put the toast on the grill and the beans in the pot.

He read. She watched.

He put the letter down. He shook his head.

"I had no idea...poor Deirdre. Get the skewer and nail me to the wall."

"Don't tempt me."

"I really am sorry." He took her in his arms and she wept for Deirdre.

They smelt the toast and beans burning.

"Aah ambrosia!" he said. "Where's the Chanel?"